BEYOND
THE MAGIC
SPHERE

BEYOND THE MAGIC SPHERE

Gail Jarrow

Jane Yolen Books
Harcourt Brace & Company
San Diego   New York   London

Requests for permission to make copies
of any part of the work should be mailed to:
Permissions Department, Harcourt Brace & Company,
6277 Sea Harbor Drive, Orlando, Florida 32887-6777.

Library of Congress Cataloging-in-Publication Data
Jarrow, Gail.
Beyond the magic sphere / by Gail Jarrow. — 1st ed.
p.   cm.
"Jane Yolen books."
Summary: Away from her city routine, eleven-year-old S.B. gets
caught up in a new friend's story of magic and intrigue, and learns
to view life differently.
ISBN 0-15-200193-X
[1. Fantasy games—Fiction.   2. Country life—Fiction.]
I. Title.
PZ7.J2955Be   1994
[Fic]—dc20   94-6884

This text was set in Granjon.

Designed by Trina Stahl

Printed in the United States of America

First edition

A B C D E

FOR TATE

Contents

BEYOND THE MAGIC SPHERE

1

Skunks and Turkeys

THE MINUTE S.B. stepped off the plane she knew that she'd been tricked. Deceived. Duped. Her father had given her a slick sales pitch over the Memorial Day weekend, and she'd been stupid enough to fall for it.

"The college has a special music program for kids your age," he had said. "It's one of the best in the state. You can work on your violin all summer."

"But I don't want to work on my violin all summer," S.B. had said. "I want to go to Europe with you."

"In the afternoons you'll be able to swim," her father went on, ignoring S.B.'s comment. "The lake is beautiful. I spent a weekend sailing and waterskiing there once. And the city is quite interesting. It'll be fun."

"Not as fun as ParisLondonCopenhagenRomeMadridAthensLisbonZurich," argued S.B.

"You'd get tired of all the traveling after the first week," said her father. "I'll be spending most of the time doing business. You know how it is with all those late meetings and dinners. The music program will be more interesting for you than trotting around with me for a month."

"I'd rather go to Grammy's. Or even to Lydia's camp."

"Grammy's health hasn't been good, S.B.," her father said. "It wouldn't work out for you to go there. Besides, since I'll be out of the country, I'll feel better knowing that you're with Brenda."

"But why Brenda? I've never even met her," said S.B.

"You'll like her. She's a real peach," he replied. "I think you'll have an exciting vacation."

"How can a place that only rates a teeny, tiny, microscopic dot on the New York State map be exciting?" she said. "The roads into it are thin blue lines. *Blue,* not even red."

"It's big enough to have an airport," her father had assured her.

Some airport. Now that she'd seen it, S.B. realized that her father had used the word loosely. The place was smaller than her school cafeteria. One anemic ceiling fan. One phone booth from the Dark Ages, out of order. One ladies' room, out of order. One, and only one, baggage handler, who had tossed her luggage through a little door onto the floor of the building.

As her taxi left the airport's parking lot, S.B. had a feeling she might be in for more unpleasant surprises.

For some reason, Brenda the Peach hadn't shown up at the airport. Even though taking a taxi wasn't a big deal to S.B.—living in the city, she was used to that—it bothered her that no one had come to meet her. She couldn't understand why her father had shipped her off to stay with this stranger. And Brenda *was* a stranger, even if he claimed she was some terrific and marvelous relative.

"Umph!" she cried as she was jolted out of her seat into the painfully solid roof of the taxi.

"Sorry about that," said the driver. "There are some monster potholes on these roads. I didn't see that one in time."

So this is what blue lines on a road map are like, S.B. thought as she rubbed the tender spot on the top of her head. Winding, narrow, and bumpy.

"Friend of mine hit a deer here last fall," the driver said as they passed another animal crossing sign. "Bad place for them. You're not from around here, are you?"

"No," said S.B., cranking open the window to catch the breeze.

"I didn't think so. Everyone getting off the planes from New York City has that same pasty skin color. Must be the air pollution that does it."

"Yuck." S.B. quickly closed her window. "You've got some air pollution problems yourselves."

"That's wood pussy. Skunk." He laughed. "Something must have made it mad."

The taxi turned onto a dirt road and stopped suddenly. "Here we are," said the driver. "Two hundred Turkey Hill Road. This is a big area for wild turkeys. If you're lucky, you'll see one."

"This can't be right," said S.B., staring out the window. The house was surrounded by trees — big trees and lots of them, a whole forest of them, in fact. "It's supposed to be in the city. Near the lake."

"Well, you're miles away from them. But this is it. See for yourself." The driver pointed to the mailbox.

Crudely painted on the rusty mailbox, nowhere near the lake and the city where she had expected to spend her summer, was the same address she'd found under Brenda's name in the phone book at the airport.

He *had* tricked her.

Brenda's house wasn't at all what S.B. had envisioned. It was old. Not quaint-and-tastefully-restored old. Not falling-apart-and-rundown old. Just *plain* old. The roof of the two-story house was a faded green, and the wooden siding was the color of dirty snow. Nailed to the porch railing was a hand-painted sign that said BOOS AND BAL-LOONS.

Mounted on a pedestal in the middle of the grass was a glass globe the size of a basketball. Pink and white flowers grew around its base. Beside the narrow stone footpath that led from the driveway to the porch stood a two-foot-high wooden figure—a rear view of a fat woman, complete with chubby legs and an expansive behind neatly painted with red polka dots. S.B. wondered whether Grammy would have another heart attack if she found out that one of her relatives had such tacky ornaments on her lawn.

"That'll be eight dollars," said the taxi driver, as he unloaded her bags from the trunk. "I hope you have it on you, because it doesn't look like anybody's home and I have to be downtown by three-thirty."

S.B. thrust the money into his hand. Grabbing her suitcase, tote bag, and violin case, she headed up the driveway to the house.

"Hey, have a good time," the driver called after her.

"Not likely," replied S.B. Then she watched as the taxi rumbled down the road and disappeared in a puff of dirt, leaving her alone with the skunks and turkeys.

2

The Lawn Lady

Hello?" S.B. CALLED through the screen door.

Although it was shadowy inside, she could make out a sofa, a chair, a television, and a stereo. The room was neat and uncluttered. No magazines scattered all over or empty beverage cans lying on the floor. That was a point in Brenda's favor, even if she did have a tasteless front yard and was rude enough to leave a guest stranded at the airport.

A disturbing thought crept into S.B.'s mind as she stared through the screen. Maybe Brenda hadn't shown up at the airport because she wasn't too eager to see S.B. Maybe the woman didn't want her to stay for the summer. Maybe she'd told S.B.'s father, "Jon, don't you dare send that kid here. If you do, I'll make her life miserable." But her father had done it anyway, because he wanted to go to Europe without her.

S.B. could tell that the door wasn't locked from the way it moved when she knocked. But she didn't think she should open it. You didn't barge into someone's house without an invitation, especially if you weren't particularly welcome.

She decided to look around back. Leaving her bags and violin case on the porch, she walked down the stone footpath to the driveway. Attached to the rear of the house was a carport. The walls were made of row after row of firewood, stacked solidly from ground to roof. Parked between them was a red pickup truck.

A streak of movement caught her eye. S.B. cautiously peeked around the corner of the carport's rear wall. What other kinds of creatures lurked in these woods? Skunks and wild turkeys were bad enough. She hoped it wasn't bear country.

She noticed a grove of evergreen trees several yards behind the house. Hanging on a rope strung between the trunks of the trees were four flapping white sheets. In the middle of the trees and sheets was a life-sized lawn ornament leaning over a wicker basket, her broad rear end covered by red shorts.

The lawn lady straightened up and reached for one of the sheets on the clothesline.

"Hello?" S.B. called. The lawn lady didn't seem to hear. "Hello," she yelled louder, as she walked across the grass toward the evergreen trees.

The woman turned around. When she saw S.B., her mouth dropped open and her eyes squinted into slits.

"I'm sorry if I scared you," said S.B., going no closer.

The lawn lady cocked her head. Then her perplexed expression stretched into a grin nearly as wide as her bottom. She pulled a set of earphones from her head and bolted across the grass toward S.B.

The sight of an elephant-sized woman charging toward her was a hundred times more terrifying than the bumpy ride in the commuter plane from New York City. Closing her eyes, S.B. braced herself for the impact. Seconds later, she was encircled by two meaty arms and lost somewhere in the folds of the lawn lady's loose-fitting blouse.

"Are you Brenda?" S.B. croaked as she wriggled

out of the clinch. She had to be, of course. Still, this woman, who was at least as tall as S.B.'s father, was nothing like the "peach" he had called her. Peaches were small, soft, and velvety. Brenda was bulky, solid, and rough. Her brown hair was heaped in a curly mass that rose from her head like a drum major's hat. Her face was creased with wrinkles. Definitely not a peach. More like a pineapple.

"S.B.!" cried Brenda. "We've been waiting for you."

Afraid that this might be the prelude to another gut-squashing hug, S.B. stepped back.

"But you're early," said Brenda, without attempting another embrace.

"The flight was rescheduled last week. My dad told you, didn't he?" said S.B., not sure whether to be relieved that Brenda seemed glad to see her or annoyed that she'd been left waiting at the airport.

"Why, no," said Brenda, shaking her head. "Oh my, what a mix-up! How did you ever get from the airport?"

"I took a taxi," replied S.B. So, it had been her *father* who'd botched the plans, not Brenda.

"A taxi!" Brenda put her hands on her bountiful hips and shook her head. "An eleven-year-old shouldn't come into a strange town all alone. Why didn't you call me from the airport?"

"The phone there didn't work. Besides," said S.B., raising her chin and trying not to reveal her concern that Brenda hadn't wanted her, "I'm used to traveling alone. I've been flying to Grammy's in Florida by myself since I was five."

"Well, the important thing," said Brenda, "is that you've arrived. And I'm tickled pink."

Then, before S.B. saw the onslaught coming, Brenda had flung an arm around her shoulders and swept her toward the house.

S.B. felt more secure with four walls and a roof between her and the skunks, turkeys, and bears. She followed Brenda up the creaky staircase to the second floor.

"You said *'We*'ve been waiting,'" she commented as Brenda stopped at the top of the stairs to catch her breath.

"Finis and I," the Pineapple replied. She motioned to the first room on the left. "The bathroom's there. Your towel is on the rack behind the door."

"Who's Finis?" asked S.B.

"He lives with me."

"Is he your husband?"

Brenda laughed. The laugh sounded as if it came from a pit deep inside her. "No, not my husband."

S.B. cringed. She wondered if Grammy knew about this detail of Brenda's life-style. Tacky lawn ornaments were one thing, but a live-in boyfriend was quite another. "Does my father know about him?"

"Of course," said Brenda. "Didn't he tell you?"

"No," replied S.B. What else hadn't her father told her about this place?

"You'll meet him soon. He's never late for dinner." With her foot, Brenda pushed open one of the two doors at the end of the short hall. "This will be your room. Nothing fancy, but the mattress is comfortable."

It was tidy, just as the living room had been, and bright. The two windows were framed with white frilly curtains. A twin bed took up most of the floor space. Beside it sat a small table with a yellow lamp. A wooden bureau with attached mirror stood in the corner. At least the accommodations are decent, thought S.B.

"See this bedspread?" Brenda asked as she put the suitcase by the closet. "It was made by my grandmother. Your great-grandmother."

"You mean Grammy's mother?" asked S.B., as

she stepped around the foot of the bed and placed her violin and tote bag next to the bureau.

"That's right. Your dad is my first cousin. Your grammy and my mother are sisters, you know."

"Oh." S.B. hadn't known. No one had bothered to explain it before. She felt a little better, seeing exactly how Brenda fit into the family tree. "So you're my aunt or something."

"More like your cousin. And if you call me Auntie, I'll turn you into a soufflé." She laughed that pit-deep laugh again, and her mass of hair jiggled like jello. "And what about you? Should I call you S.B. or St—"

"S.B.," she said quickly. "I never use the other."

"Why not? It's such a pretty name," said Brenda. "And with your hair and freckles—"

"I don't like it," S.B. interrupted. "It's silly, and I'm going to change it legally when I'm older. My father said I could."

"Did he?" Brenda smoothed the bedspread with her hand. S.B. detected a change in Brenda's voice. It sounded soft and smooth, not prickly like a pineapple.

"You look just like your mother," said Brenda. "Same nose and mouth, same thick auburn hair. But I'm sure your dad has told you that before."

S.B. shook her head. "He never mentioned it."

He never mentioned anything about her mother. She wished that Brenda hadn't.

Brenda smiled. "I'm glad that you decided to stay with us this summer."

S.B. glanced across the room at her cousin. *Pineapple* wasn't quite the right description for Brenda. She wasn't wrinkly and ugly. Those lines at the corners of her eyes and mouth were from grinning. *Pineapple* was all wrong, really. Brenda was more like a pumpkin.

"I'm going to enjoy having you around," said Brenda, her face crinkled by her smile.

The next thing S.B. knew, Brenda had encased her in another mummy-tight hug. Of all the luck, she thought as she gasped for air. Four long weeks with an affectionate jack-o'-lantern.

3

Request Denied

BRENDA HAD BEEN right about Finis. He
came home about the same time as the smells of
dinner began to drift up from the kitchen into
S.B.'s room.

When she heard the back screen door snap
shut, S.B. placed her last pair of shorts in the bureau. Grabbing the gift her father wanted her to
give Brenda, she hurried downstairs. She couldn't
wait to see what kind of man would fall in love
with a pumpkin.

Since she hadn't yet had a tour of the downstairs, S.B. followed the cooking smells and sound

of voices to the rear of the house. She stopped in her tracks when she came to the dining room.

Unlike the neat and orderly living room, this room looked like the aftermath of a three-year-old's birthday party. Scores of balloons—red, yellow, green, blue, silver—floated against the ceiling. The attached strings dangled from the colorful cloud, like white stalactites in a cave. A large table in the center of the room was covered with cards, ribbons, and baskets. Several boxes were piled in the corner near the window, and the floor around the table was littered with paper and bits of ribbon. Next to the Mickey Mouse phone at the end of the table sat a huge hairy gorilla slumped in a chair, its eyes gazing vacantly at S.B.

"He's my Boo costume," said Brenda, appearing in the doorway. "We call him Tarzan." She took S.B. by the hand and pulled her into the kitchen. "And this is another inhabitant of the house. We call him Finis Hatcher."

Leaning against the sink stood a long-legged boy as narrow as Brenda was broad. Water dripped from his curly brown hair. He was a couple of inches taller than S.B., and she guessed that he was a year or two older. He wore frayed cutoffs and a baggy T-shirt. He looked at S.B. the way a picnicker looks at a rain cloud.

"Finis, this is S.B. Field," said Brenda, as she put a pot on the counter beside him. "And kindly don't use my vegetable sprayer to rinse your face next time."

"Okay, okay," the boy mumbled.

"I don't get it," said S.B., glancing at Brenda. "I . . . I thought Finis was your significant other."

" 'Significant other'!" Finis wiped the water from his face. "Is she for real?"

"Finis is like you," said Brenda, pulling a platter of chicken from the oven. "He's my cousin's son—on my father's side, instead of on my mother's side, the way you are. He's been living with me since last summer."

"Oh," replied S.B., feeling more in the dark than ever. First she found out that she would be sharing Brenda's house with a mystery man. Then the mystery man turned out to be a boy. But why did he live here? She could see that Brenda wasn't going to explain, and it didn't seem polite to ask. Remembering the present in her hands, S.B. thrust it toward Brenda. "This is for having me."

"Thank you, S.B." Brenda tore off the wrapping paper. "We'll have to call your father right after dinner. He'll want to know that you arrived safely."

"Good idea," replied S.B. She had plenty she wanted to talk to him about.

"Look, Finis, a pasta maker. How nice!" Brenda exclaimed. "Your father remembers the way to my heart, S.B."

"He said you liked to cook." S.B. stole a glimpse at Finis, who happened to be stealing a glimpse at her. They both looked away quickly.

Brenda placed the pasta maker on the top of the refrigerator and handed S.B. a plate. "We're informal here," she said. "Help yourself."

S.B. stepped over to the counter, where Finis stood heaping chicken, rice, and peas onto his plate. As she finished getting her food, an arm reached over her shoulder and plopped another spoonful of rice on her plate.

"I'll have none of that anorexia business in my house," said Brenda. "You eat less than a hamster. I'm going to fatten you up this summer."

"That's what the witch told Hansel," said Finis.

"You keep out of this." With her free hand, Brenda mussed up his hair.

After they all sat down at the kitchen table, Brenda smiled and said, "Enjoy." S.B. realized that this was the signal to dig in, because Finis instantly began to wolf down his food.

"What are the balloons in the dining room for?" she asked, trying not to look at Finis, even though it was he that she was most curious about.

"That's for Boos and Balloons," explained Brenda. "It's a small business I run evenings and weekends. Gives me a break from my job at the college."

"Boos and Balloons?"

"My customers want to communicate a personal message," said Brenda. "Instead of flowers, they send balloons, which I deliver attached to wine bottles, baskets of candy, or whatever they request. Help yourself to more, S.B. There's plenty."

"I'm not finished with this yet," S.B. said, noting that Finis had already inhaled his third helping of rice.

"Then there are those people who have a less positive emotion to express," said Brenda.

"Remember that guy whose wife ran off with his best friend?" said Finis.

He and Brenda snickered. "That's where the boos come in," she said. "For them I deliver cream pies in the face, wet blankets, insulting limericks, and bags of manure."

"Horse, cow, or sheep," added Finis.

"What?" S.B. choked on a mouthful of peas.

"Horse, cow, or sheep manure. Depends on what we can get." He grinned.

"Maybe you'd like to help while you're here, S.B.," said Brenda.

No way, she thought, picturing herself in a cow pasture, shoveling manure into bags.

"How about swimming?" asked Brenda.

"What about it?" S.B. pushed her peas around her plate with her fork. She had lost her appetite somewhere between Finis's mouthful of rice and the bagful of manure.

"Finis can take you tomorrow. It's supposed to be a hot day."

Finis made an unenthusiastic grunt and continued to stuff food into his mouth.

S.B. put down her fork. "But I'll be starting violin camp tomorrow."

"Oh my." Brenda reached across the table and touched S.B.'s arm. "Didn't your father explain? The program was all filled by the time he asked me to sign you up. You were on the waiting list, but when I called Friday, they said there weren't any cancellations. So there's no opening."

S.B. jerked her arm away from Brenda's hand. "What do you mean, 'no opening'? What's the point of being here if I can't go to violin camp?"

Finis stopped eating and stared at her. Brenda looked bewildered. "I thought you knew about this."

It was all too much for S.B. She could forgive her father for misleading her about the city and the lake. She could probably put up with the dirt road and the forest of lurking beasts. She could overlook the tacky lawn ornaments and the gorilla in the dining room. She might even be able to tolerate a boy who ate like a vacuum cleaner and a woman who was the Avon lady of cow manure. But to be stuck here with absolutely nothing to do for four weeks—twenty-eight long, interminable days—was torture. Cruel and unusual punishment.

"I need to call my father immediately." She pushed back her chair.

"But you haven't eaten anything," said Brenda.

"I'm not hungry." S.B. headed for the phone on the dining room table beside the gorilla. Picking up Mickey Mouse's ears, she dialed the apartment in New York. Her father answered on the third ring.

"It's your daughter," said S.B. "Remember me?"

"Hi, S.B. Flight go okay?"

"You forgot to tell Brenda about the flight change," she muttered.

"I asked my secretary to do that for me last week," he replied. "Oh well. You got there all right, didn't you?"

He should have called himself, thought S.B. bitterly. "You didn't tell me what they were like."

She turned her back to Tarzan the gorilla. "Or what this place was like."

"Brenda's terrific, isn't she?"

"Nothing's the way you said it would be. And I can't get into violin camp."

"I'd hoped that a position would open up for you."

His calm tone of voice made S.B. angry. He didn't seem to care whether she went to violin camp or not. "There'll be nothing to do if I don't have violin camp. I'll go crazy. I *have* to come with you to Europe."

"I want you to stay with Brenda," he said. "It's important to me."

"How about what's important to me?" S.B. cried. She realized her voice was loud and that Brenda and Finis could hear her. She didn't care. "I don't want to stay here."

"It's the best thing for you, S.B.," he said. "Trust me on this."

He made her summer vacation sound like an inoculation. *It'll hurt, but it's good for you.* "I don't mind about missing violin camp," she told her father. "I could learn more traveling with you."

"I'll call you in a few days," he said.

"But what about Europe?"

"I'll send you plenty of postcards with pretty stamps."

Postcards! Did he think that would make up for the pain and suffering she was being forced to endure? Slamming the phone down without saying good-bye, S.B. ran upstairs to her room.

How could he do this to her? Leave her in a place where the tallest structures for miles were trees. Abandon her while he had a great time in Europe. She didn't belong here.

He had lured her into the trap. He'd known all along about the violin camp and where Brenda lived and even about Finis. And he hadn't told her because he realized that if she'd known, she would have refused to get on that plane. Instead he had deceived her. Lied to her.

Now she was stuck ... trapped ... as if she had fallen into wet cement. And the cement was hardening, encasing her like one of Brenda's embraces.

4

A Day with the King of Gruesome Trivia

THE NEXT MORNING when S.B. came down for breakfast, she found Finis at the kitchen table. "Where's Brenda?" she asked him.

"At work." Finis didn't bother looking up from his book, which was propped against the orange-juice container.

"What does she do at the college, anyway?"

"She's an assistant to a professor," replied Finis.

"What kind of professor?"

"An art historian who studies the doodles around the page borders of medieval books," said Finis, gulping some juice. "Any *more* questions?"

24

"Well, excu-u-use me," said S.B., "but nobody told me anything about her—or you."

"You have to get your own breakfast."

S.B. looked around the kitchen. She felt as if she'd been dropped onto an alien planet. Everything here was different and strange. She didn't know the rules. She didn't understand the natives. She didn't know how she was expected to act. And she didn't know which cupboard held the cereal.

A considerate person would have helped her feel at ease by showing her where things were. But S.B. had seen enough to know that Finis wasn't likely to do that. Rather than awkwardly search through the cupboards while he stared at her, she took a bagel off the plate on the table.

"Could I have some juice, please?" she said to Finis.

"Take it."

"Your book is resting against the container."

He snatched the book away.

"Did you know I was coming this summer?" she asked as she poured her juice.

"Yeah, and it was pretty depressing news, too."

"What do you know about me?" She put the container back in front of him.

"That you're a spoiled brat."

"I am not!"

"When Daddy won't give in, you throw a tantrum. Sounds spoiled to me."

"If you're talking about last night—well, you don't know the whole story. He tricked me into coming here. It wasn't fair."

Finis shrugged. "Sure."

"It wasn't! You wouldn't understand. You live here." S.B. broke off a piece of bagel. "I'm not staying. There's no way I'm staying. I'm going to Europe with my father."

"Europe? I bet you've never heard about the Great Plague of London." Finis laid his book on the table. For the first time S.B. noticed that the illustration on the cover was of a swarm of red-eyed rats. "It killed off a third of the population," he said.

"I'm not interested in plagues," muttered S.B. This table conversation was even worse than the one about manure.

"The plague in the third century was another major outbreak," Finis continued. "Five thousand Romans died every day."

"If you don't mind," said S.B., "I'm eating."

"Suit yourself." Pushing back his chair, Finis picked up the rat-covered book and carried his plate to the sink. He brushed past S.B. and grabbed a raincoat from the hook by the back door.

"Where are you going?" she asked, trying not to sound as if she cared.

"None of your business."

S.B. glanced out the window at the rain splashing in puddles on the driveway. "When will you be back?"

"When I get back." Slamming the screen door behind him, Finis was gone.

And S.B. was left alone. Just like at home.

For several minutes, she stared at the kitchen clock. Another example of Brenda's odd sense of decorating, it was the shape of a black cat, with arms pointing to the numbers as its swinging tail clicked off the seconds.

The house was quiet except for the click-clicking of the clock-cat's tail and the drip-dripping of the rain. There wasn't a trace of background noise. No car horns or truck mufflers or shouting voices. S.B. wasn't used to such silence. It made her feel even lonelier.

She felt skittish, too, as if rubber bands were stretching and snapping inside of her. What was she supposed to do all day?

She tried to remember what she did at home on rainy days with nothing on her schedule. But she couldn't recall a day like that. Free time was not an area in which S.B. had had much experience. Something was always planned. Violin

lessons, tennis lessons, swim lessons, choir, Girl
Scouts, gymnastics, ice-skating. Her previous summer vacations had always been more of the same,
with the activities lengthened to last all day.

It wasn't as if S.B. actually had fun doing
these things. In fact, some of them were pretty
awful, especially the sports-related ones. Maybe it
wouldn't have been so bad if her father had let
her choose for herself what she did. Still, her time
was filled. That, she supposed, was the whole
point. She wished that she had something to fill
her time now.

She noticed some books lying around. But
they looked boring. She didn't feel like reading
anyway. There was television, of course. Her father called it The Great Mind Anesthetizer. He
didn't let her watch anything but PBS. She
headed for the living room, casting an uncomfortable glance at Tarzan the gorilla as she passed
through the dining room.

A spin through the television dial turned up
only static and snow. Her father could rest easy.
Her mind would not be numbed, at least not by
Brenda's broken television. By boredom, yes. S.B.
wasn't sure how long she could stand the rubber
bands stretching and snapping inside her.

The Mickey Mouse phone in the dining room
rang. The sudden sound made her jump. But the

promise of hearing someone's voice sent S.B. running to answer it.

The machine beat her. "Boos and Balloons. Creative insults and innovative kudos," said Brenda's prerecorded voice. "I can't come to the phone at the moment. Please leave your name and number, and I'll get back to you."

S.B. stood listening as the caller recited his name and phone number. Even the phone calls are boring, she thought as she climbed the stairs to the second floor.

She stopped outside Finis's room at the end of the hall. His door was shut tight. S.B. had an uncontrollable urge to open it. At the very moment her brain was reminding her how rude it was to snoop, her hand was turning the doorknob. It was locked. Disappointed and annoyed, she went into her own room and flopped on the bed.

Her pillow smelled like a Christmas tree. She quickly reminded herself that fragrant sheets weren't enough to make her like Brenda or this house in the middle of nowhere. She hated her father for sending her here. When he called, she would refuse to talk to him. She'd tear up his postcards and burn the pretty stamps. She'd make him feel as miserable as she felt.

S.B. watched the clock's red digital numbers change. 9:47 . . . 9:48 . . . 9:49. The rain seemed to be letting up. 9:50 ... 9:51 ... 9:52. The yarn of the bedspread itched. She rolled off the bed. The rubber bands stretched and snapped. S.B. fidgeted. She rearranged the contents of the top bureau drawer. She lined up her shoes in a different order.

Finally, when she could think of nothing else to do, she opened her violin case and pulled out the music that her teacher had told her to practice over the summer. She liked practicing about as much as she liked educational television, but at least it was a way to kill some time.

Sitting on the bed, she propped her music against the lamp on the bedside table and began to play. At the end of the first page, she stopped, suddenly aware of someone behind her. Finis stood in the doorway, his hands stuffed in the pockets of his cutoffs.

"How long have you been playing that thing?" he said.

"Five years," S.B. replied, using her most condescending tone of voice.

Finis shook his head. "Too bad you have such a lousy teacher."

"He's not a lousy teacher," objected S.B., before she realized that he was insulting *her*.

"I guess that's why you wanted to come here for that music camp," he continued.

"Music camp wasn't my idea. But at least that would have been better than being stuck with you." S.B. glared at him. "My father tricked me. He forced me to come."

"Unfortunate—for both of us." Finis pushed his hair off his forehead. "Brenda says I have to take you swimming today. The rain stopped. Let's go." He turned and stalked down the hallway.

Going swimming with a person as rude and unfriendly as Finis was not S.B.'s idea of a wonderful time. Still, it was a notch above practicing and two notches above being alone and doing nothing. She tossed her violin on the bed and dug through the bureau for her bathing suit.

She found Finis outside, waiting for her in the driveway. Still wearing his cutoffs, he had taken off his shirt. He tossed her a towel and an apple. She caught the towel but dropped the apple. It rolled along the gravel, landing at the edge of the grass.

"Oh gross! It smashed a worm," she cried. She gingerly picked the apple up by its stem. "It's covered with worm guts."

"Good. You'll have a nutritionally balanced snack," said Finis, as he crunched down the gravel driveway to the road.

S.B. considered throwing the apple into the woods. But because she was hungry, she rolled it

in the wet grass instead and rinsed off the slime
as best she could.

By that time Finis had turned up the dirt road
and was out of sight. S.B. ran to catch him.
"Where's the pool?" she asked. He had a long
stride. She had to jog to keep up.

"Two miles away, and we don't belong to it."

"A lake?" she said, hoping that there might be
one closer than the distant blue strip she'd seen
from the taxi.

"Even farther."

"Then where are we going?" S.B. was out of
breath from running after him.

"You'll see when we get there."

They came to a large, broad-leafed tree. Its
thick branches spread over the road as if they
were grabbing at something on the other side.
The twisted trunk, wrapped with vines, reminded
S.B. of a spiral staircase.

Finis pointed to the vines. "Watch out for the
poison ivy." He stepped to the edge of the road
and jumped the ditch.

S.B. watched him disappear into the bushes.
She wasn't thrilled by the looks of the woods. Too
dark. Too mysterious. She liked to know where
she was going and what was going to happen
when she got there. This looked like a place to be

avoided. She wondered if Finis might be tricking her. Maybe there wasn't anywhere to swim in these woods, after all. She didn't trust him.

Still, she was hot and sweaty, especially after trekking up the hill. The mosquitoes and black flies, attracted by her perspiration, were eating her alive. She didn't want to miss the chance to cool off if there really was a place to swim.

"Aren't you coming?" called Finis from some-where among the trees. "Or are you afraid?"

"Of course I'm not afraid," said S.B., swal-lowing hard and leaping across the ditch. She held her towel in front of her like a shield and plowed into the vegetation. After ten paces, the thick brush gave way to a path through the trees. Finis had waited for her, but as soon as she came close, he took off down the path. S.B. hurried after him.

"There are thirty-seven species of North American animals that carry plague," he called back to her. "Foxes, bobcats, even dogs and house cats. Any of them could be right here in these woods, S.B. Think of it."

She was trying very hard not to. "You're not scaring me, if that's what you're trying to do," she said, panting as she followed him down the path.

"And then there's the ticks. They carry several nasty diseases. Got to watch out for them." He quickened his pace. "Lots of owls around here, too. Vicious birds. You should see them tear a mouse apart."

"Sounds lovely," muttered S.B.

"The next full moon, when it's shadowy and spooky, I'll take you owling." He grinned at her over his shoulder. "I bet you'd enjoy that."

When he turned around, she stuck out her tongue at his back.

Finis stopped several yards ahead. "Here we are."

"This is it?" said S.B. "It's only a stream." Her father had promised her a summer on the water, and this was what she got.

"I dammed it up last summer," said Finis, pointing to a pile of rocks downstream. "After a rain, like today, is the best time."

S.B. looked at the brown water. "What about over there?" she said, pointing down the hill. "Isn't the water clearer somewhere else?"

"The stream runs into Old Ogden's land," said Finis. "He doesn't like anyone on his property. Once when he saw me, he made a big deal about it to Brenda." He tore off his sneakers. "Besides, the water's deeper here. Better swimming."

S.B. laid her shoes, towel, and apple on one of the large boulders bordering the stream. She wondered what the bottom would feel like. She hoped it would have smooth pebbles instead of squishy mud.

She watched Finis wade into the stream. The water came up to his chest. Climbing down to the water's edge, she stuck in a toe. A refreshing coolness instantly spread through her body.

"Oh, I forgot to tell you," Finis called from the middle of the stream. "Don't worry about the leeches. I know how to pull them off."

"Leeches?" S.B. yanked her foot out of the water.

"You know. Those flat black worms that swell up when they suck your blood." He dove under the water.

S.B. thought about having black, slimy suckers clinging to her skin. She wasn't sure if Finis was lying to her, but she didn't want to take any chances. She retreated to the rock.

Finis's head broke through the surface of the gurgling water. "Aren't you coming in? Temperature's perfect."

"Maybe later," S.B. said weakly. "I think I'll eat my apple first." After rubbing the apple with her towel (in case there were a few stray pieces of worm gut left), S.B. took a bite. It was nice and juicy, one of the best apples she'd had in a while.

She watched Finis make dolphin dives to the opposite bank. She could tell that he was a strong swimmer. Swimming back again, he pulled himself up on the boulder nearest her. She scanned his body for leeches, hoping to see one—nice and juicy—sucking *his* blood. But there was none.

Finis glanced over at her and grinned. Then he jumped off the rock, cannonballing into the middle of the stream. A shower of muddy water thoroughly drenched her. "I thought you could use some cooling off," he said when his head emerged from the water.

S.B. shook the drops from her half-eaten apple. Finis seemed determined to make her miserable. "Hey, what happened to your parents, Minus Finis?" she said, hoping that he had been dumped off with Brenda the way she had. Abandoned. Discarded like an unwanted piece of furniture. It would serve him right.

"They're dead."

"Oh," said S.B. It was a disappointment. She hadn't wanted to feel sorry for him. "How did they die?"

"They got sick. One cancer. One heart. Bing. Bang. That's all, folks." He climbed out of the water.

"How old were you?" asked S.B.

"Want to know something? You're driving me crazy with all your questions." He leaped to the rock where she sat. "How about staying out of my business?"

S.B. felt his wet knees against her back. Cold water dripped from his body onto her shoulders.

"Do you know why they called the plague the Black Death?" he asked in a slow, sinister voice, like someone reading a ghost story.

"No," said S.B., "and I don't care."

"It was because the tongues of the infected people turned black."

Pretending not to listen, S.B. continued to munch her apple.

"They spit up blood and had high fevers. But the worst part was"—he leaned down close to her ear—"the swellings. Excruciating black hemorrhages all over the body. Swellings as big as . . . apples!"

S.B. jumped to her feet and tossed her apple into the stream. "You did that just to be mean!" she screamed, immediately regretting that she'd reacted to his trick.

Finis laughed. "Can't you take a joke?"

S.B. had had enough of Finis and his swimming hole. Collecting her towel and shoes, she scrambled off the rock.

"Watch out for the ticks," he called.

With his laughter burning in her ears, S.B. dashed through the woods to the road, hoping that none of the thirty-seven species of plague carriers was lurking behind the next tree.

5

Water, Earth, and the Magic Sphere

How's this?" said Finis.

July Four means red, white, and blue.
Fireworks go off when I think of you.

The three of them—four counting Tarzan the gorilla—sat around the dining room table, filling wicker baskets with tiny flags and red-white-and-blue lollipops.

"I like it," said Brenda the Pumpkin, as she tied a red ribbon. "We could stick a box of sparklers in each basket. What do you think, S.B.?"

S.B. wasn't about to compliment Finis even if it had been a clever poem, which it wasn't. "It's okay," she said flatly.

Brenda pushed herself out of the chair. She circled the table, examining the ceiling and occasionally grabbing one of the many strings dangling above their heads until she had a handful of colorful balloons. S.B. thought that she looked like someone plucking a bouquet of flowers from a garden.

"We'll go with it, Finis," said Brenda, as she deftly attached the bouquet of balloons to the basket. "You can type up a few cards tomorrow."

"What about me?" asked S.B.

"I hope you'll want to help, too," said Brenda. "Finis can show you how to fill the balloons with helium. Or maybe you'll try your hand at some poems. We can always use new ideas. Innovation—that's what makes Boos and Balloons successful."

"I didn't mean that," said S.B. "I meant, what about this summer? What am I supposed to do tomorrow? And the twenty-six tomorrows after that?"

"Relax and rest up for school," said Brenda, as she arranged lollipops in the basket. "That's what summers are for."

"How can I relax? Your TV doesn't work, and you don't even have a VCR," grumbled S.B.

"Don't tell me that thing's acting up again." Brenda shook her head.

"My father won't like me wasting time."

"Who says you'll be wasting time?" asked Brenda.

"But there's nothing to do around here," said S.B.

"Nothing to do?" Brenda looked down the table at Finis. "Didn't you take S.B. swimming today, like I asked you?"

"Yeah, I took her," said Finis, "and I'm not going to do it again. I'm not baby-sitting her anymore."

"Baby-sitting!" S.B. exclaimed. "I don't need a baby-sitter—certainly not someone as depraved as you."

"What's this about?" asked Brenda.

Finis glared at S.B. "She expected a sparkling blue concrete pool for her dainty feet."

"That's right," said S.B., glaring back. "And a lake with sailing and water skiing, and a city with plays and concerts. And a nice place to stay, without demented boys who constantly talk about disgusting things." She knew it was rude to say this in front of Brenda, but she didn't feel obligated to her father to use good manners, considering what he'd gotten her into.

"Oh my." Brenda shook her head. Her pumpkin grin and smiling creases were gone. "I suppose this isn't exactly what you're used to, S.B." She clicked her tongue and shook her head again. "Maybe if we introduced you to another girl your age."

"No," snapped Finis. "Not Cally."

"Who's Cally?" asked S.B.

"She lives up the hill, at the end of the road." Brenda's smile creases reappeared. "I don't know why I didn't think of this before."

"Cally's not her type," said Finis.

"Why don't you let Cally and S.B. decide that?" said Brenda.

Finis threw his pen onto the table and stomped out of the room.

"What are we going to do about him, Tarzan?" Brenda sighed as an upstairs door slammed shut.

S.B. knew what she'd like to do about him.

"Finis can take you up to Cally's tomorrow," said Brenda. "He'll be out of his funk by then."

"I doubt it," mumbled S.B. "He doesn't like me. And he doesn't want me here."

"You two need some time to get used to each other, that's all."

"Yeah, at least a millennium." S.B. jammed a flag into the basket in front of her. "Why does he live with you, anyway?"

"I'm the closest relative he has," said Brenda. "His parents were much older than I am. They had Finis late in life. His grandparents are gone, too. I'm lucky to have him."

"Lucky?" It seemed like *bad* luck to S.B.

"Yes, lucky." Brenda reached across the table and patted S.B.'s hand with her sweaty palm. "Don't jump to conclusions about Finis. He's a sheep in wolf's clothing."

It didn't matter to S.B. whether he was a sheep or wolf. She didn't like any sort of animal, particularly the kind around 200 Turkey Hill Road.

As it turned out, S.B. didn't need Finis to introduce her to Cally. The girl appeared at the back door the next morning, soon after Brenda left for work. S.B. was finishing her breakfast when the screen creaked open.

"Hi," said her visitor, settling down at the kitchen table as if it were her own house. She rested her bony elbows on the table. "You're the one from New York City. I'm Cally. Brenda wanted me to meet you, didn't she?"

"Well, yes. She mentioned you last night," said

S.B., putting down her glass. The girl's pale skin and white hair—whiter even than Grammy's—made her look like a ghost. S.B. had never seen a kid that blond. "Did Brenda call you this morning?"

"No. We don't have a phone."

"Oh. Then Finis must have gone up to get you."

"I haven't seen him. Where is he today?" the girl asked.

"He went out early. I don't know where," said S.B., trying to figure out how Cally knew about her.

"He probably went down to Dr. Armstrong's." Cally took a banana from the bowl on the table.

S.B. stared at her.

"Oh, it's okay," said Cally. "Brenda lets me. She doesn't think I eat enough."

"No one eats enough by Brenda's standards," said S.B., although in Cally's case she could see Brenda's point. The girl was scrawny, like a stray cat. Her shaggy hair straggled out from beneath a dingy white baseball hat that was splattered with gray and brown paint. Her faded yellow T-shirt with its worn-off lettering hung loosely on her shoulders. And her knobby legs looked like thin saplings below her purple shorts.

"Who is this Dr. Armstrong?" asked S.B.

"He lives around the corner, on Skunk Hollow Road." Cally slowly peeled the banana. "Finis does jobs for him—yard work and stuff."

"You mean there are other houses close by?" S.B. asked hopefully.

"Well, none between here and my house." Cally took a small bite of banana. "But there are some on Skunk Hollow. And Old Ogden lives down near the corner next to Dr. Armstrong. No other kids, though. Just Finis and me. And now you."

S.B. was sorry to hear that, although Cally seemed friendlier than Finis. At least she didn't discuss plagues. "What kind of doctor is he?"

"Dr. Armstrong? He's really a professor, not a doctor. He studies forensic anthropology."

"What's that?" asked S.B., forgetting in her curiosity to act as if she knew the words.

"He studies skeletons to figure out how people died. He has a lab at his house with lots of bones and body organs stored in bottles. Sometimes he lets Finis hang around and watch him work."

"I can see how that would appeal to Finis," said S.B. "Do you go there, too?"

Cally shook her head. "Only once, last year, right after Dr. Armstrong built his house. But I haven't gone back."

"Why not?"

"I don't like him much. His mouth smiles, but his eyes don't." Cally leaned over and touched S.B.'s hair.

S.B. stiffened. What kind of weird girl was this, to reach out and feel her hair like that?

Cally drew her hand away. "I wish mine was thick and long."

S.B. felt that she should say something like "Oh, yours is nice, too," except it was so obviously untrue that she knew her comment would sound fake. "Thanks," she said instead.

"Mine won't grow," said Cally, as she removed her hat. The short white hair stuck out at different lengths, as if it had been cut with pinking shears. Putting her hat back on, she glanced out the kitchen window. "Here's Finis now."

"I figured you'd show up sooner or later, Cally," said Finis, as he came in the back door. He pulled a milk carton from the refrigerator and took a gulp. "Swimming was good yesterday. Wasn't it, S.B.?" He grinned at her.

Watching him drink directly from the container made S.B. feel ill. She decided to get her milk only from unopened cartons in the future.

Cally got up and walked over to Finis. Standing next to him, she looked even smaller and more frail. The top of her head barely reached his shoulders. "Let's make her Air," she said to him. "That's how she came to us."

"No," said Finis. "I don't want her."

"Come on," Cally said, crossing the kitchen to S.B.'s side. "She'll be good. I know she will be."

"Good at what?" interjected S.B.

"It'll be better without her," repeated Finis, tossing the empty milk carton into the garbage can under the sink.

Cally took S.B.'s arm and dragged her from her chair. S.B. was surprised by her strength. She looked as if she could barely lift a handful of Brenda's balloons.

"I'm Earth," said Cally, as she pulled S.B. toward the front of the house. "Finis is Water. You'll be Air. You control the wind and breezes."

"What kind of game is this?" S.B. asked when they reached the porch.

"You'll see that I'm right, Cally." Finis had followed them outside. "You're making a major mistake."

"Three is the magic number. A third person will give us more power," said Cally. She led S.B. onto the grassy area in front of the house.

They stopped next to the glass ball that rested on the pedestal in the middle of the lawn. The surface of the ball was a smooth, seamless mirror.

Its curves bent S.B.'s image, as well as the view of Cally and the trees in the background, making everything look somehow unreal. When S.B. moved closer, her eyes seemed to bulge and her body disappeared. As she circled the ball, her reflection was constantly transformed into new distorted images.

Cally bent down and pinched off one of the pink flowers at the base of the pedestal. Holding the flower between her thumb and forefinger, she swept her arm over the ball. "Magic Sphere, Magic Sphere, we are here," she chanted. Then she laid the flower on the top of the ball and placed both her hands on its smooth sides. "You do it too, S.B.," she whispered.

S.B. shook her head and stepped away.

Finis came up behind her. To S.B.'s surprise, he placed his hands on the ball next to Cally's, and they both closed their eyes.

"The Green Lord hid the amulet in the Tangled Jungle, I am told," Cally said in a strong, deep voice sounding more like a woman's than a young girl's.

"Then to the Tangled Jungle we must go," declared Finis.

They opened their eyes and marched side by side past S.B., as though she weren't there.

"And what about Air?" Cally said.

"She was lost on the way," Finis replied. "I feared she would be."

"We could have used her power against the Green Lord's magic."

"We have achieved many quests and won many battles without it," said Finis. "And we shall do so again."

S.B. watched as the two disappeared into the trees. These kids weren't like her or any of her friends or anyone else she had ever met. She didn't belong here with them. She belonged back home, with people she could understand.

Turning away from the glass ball, S.B. hurried into the house. She hoped that Brenda's television was working. She felt like anesthetizing her brain.

6

Boos and Balloons

CALLY AND FINIS didn't come back all morning. Even though their babbling about green lords and tangled jungles had made S.B. uncomfortable, she didn't like being left behind. She had always hated that feeling.

She dreaded the evenings when her father went out to a meeting or to dinner. The door would shut behind him, and she'd watch through the window as his taxi disappeared into the night.

She hated to stay home sick and watch the other kids pass on the sidewalk on their way to school. She'd wonder all day what she was missing. What if her best friend, Lydia, shared a secret with someone else because S.B. wasn't there? Or what if the class chose partners for a project and everyone forgot about her?

Nothing was turning out right here at Brenda's. S.B. had thought that Cally would be a regular, normal girl who would keep her company until the four weeks finally ended and she could go home to civilization. Just her luck that Cally turned out to be as strange as Finis—maybe more so. To make things worse, there didn't seem to be much to do in this place except to play with glass lawn ornaments and to swim in leech-infested waters. The television didn't even work.

After wandering around the house for a while, S.B. decided to write a couple of letters. Lydia always enjoyed getting mail at camp. She might even write back. Grammy would definitely write back, returning S.B.'s letter with grammatical and spelling errors circled in red, and enclosing a crisp five-dollar bill.

S.B. found some blank paper on the dining room table under a spool of gold ribbon.

Dear Grammy,
    You should have warned me about this place. Brenda's OK, but there's a geek from another

galaxy living with her. In case you don't know what that means—he's horrible, gross, disgusting, rude, and obnoxious. Get the idea.

It's hot and there's no A/C. The humidity will probably ruin my violin. Daddy should have thought of that before he made me come here. By the way, I couldn't get into music camp because someone screwed up. But I have to stay anyway. The only swimming place is a muddy creek full of leeches, which are worse than the alligators and sharks you have in Florida because you can't see them until it's too late.

I hope your heart is feeling better.

Love
S.B.

Dear Lydia,

How's camp? Is that cute guy you liked there again this year?

Guess what? My cousin has a 13-year-old boy living with her. You should see him. He's tall with brown hair and green eyes. We have interesting conversations, and he takes me swimming. He's a good swimmer and very smart.

I talked my father out of making me go to that STUPID music camp!!!! I didn't want to waste my time inside with the violin when there's so much great stuff to do outside, like swimming and hiking.

I'm meeting lots of new kids. Brenda works all day, and I can do anything I want. She doesn't care when I go to bed. But I'm so busy that I practically collapse from exhaustion by midnight.

I'm really busy, but I'll write again if I get the chance.

Luv

S.B.

Brenda the Smiling Pumpkin called at noon to check in. "It wasn't nice of Finis to go off without you," she said when S.B. told her why Finis wasn't there. "I'll speak to him about it to-night."

"Don't do that," said S.B. "I didn't want to go with them anyhow."

"I'll be home early. My work number is on the side of the refrigerator if you need me."

"I'm fine," S.B. told her, but it wasn't true. She would be "fine" if she were in Europe with her father or at Grammy's in Florida or in camp with Lydia or *anywhere* but Brenda's house.

After Brenda's call, S.B. made herself a peanut-butter sandwich and drifted back to the dining room. The rubber bands began stretching and snapping inside her head again. It bothered her to think about Finis and Cally having fun—even if it was playing a ridiculous game—while she was stuck in the house with only an ape costume for company.

On the table next to Tarzan, she noticed the tablet that Finis had been using the previous night to compose his poem for Brenda's baskets. A pile of small gift cards lay beside it. He had promised to type up the poem, but instead he'd gone off with Cally.

Why not? thought S.B. She didn't have anything better to do. Besides, she liked to type. Her father considered it a necessary skill in the computer age and had insisted that she take a touch-typing course. It had been one of the only special programs at which S.B. had excelled. She wished that typing were an Olympic event. She could win a gold medal.

Working carefully, S.B. typed the poem onto each card. The dancing of her fingers and the tapping of the keys soon relaxed the taut rubber bands in her head. When the last card was completed, S.B. spread them out on the dining room table. They looked dull. Using a red pen she found among the clutter, she sketched a tiny firecracker in the corner of each card.

"Looks good, doesn't it, Tarzan?" she said, stepping back to admire her work. The gorilla made no comment, but what did he know? S.B. hoped that Brenda would be pleased.

By the time she placed a card in each of the Fourth of July baskets, it was nearly three o'clock. Cally and Finis hadn't returned. The television was still not working. And Tarzan didn't look like the type who would enjoy a rousing game of Monopoly.

S.B. thought about her violin resting in its padded case upstairs. That was where it was going to stay, she decided. Without her father around to insist that she practice, she intended to use the instrument only in a last, absolutely final effort to fight off boredom.

This decision made S.B. feel suddenly energetic. She ran out the front door, letting the screen slam behind her. She wanted to do something and go somewhere. But surrounded by woods full of ticks and plague carriers, she didn't have many choices. She'd have to stick to the road.

At the end of Brenda's driveway, she turned right and headed down Turkey Hill Road, skipping and kicking at small rocks as she went. When she reached the intersection with the paved road at the bottom of the hill, she heard a loud buzzing noise. Curious, she walked along the shoulder of the road, following the sound.

She passed a dented mailbox not far from the corner. A rutted dirt lane led from the road into the woods, but she could see no buildings through the trees.

Continuing farther along the paved road, to the next mailbox, she discovered the source of the buzzing. Two men with chain saws were cutting down a section of trees. A third man paced back and forth, yelling orders to them. Behind him, in the middle of a manicured lawn, sat a large house full of sparkling windows. It was the kind of house her father would like—fresh, modern, full of angles. It could have been plucked from any suburban housing development. But here on Skunk Hollow Road it seemed out of place.

After S.B. had watched for several minutes, the third man glanced toward the road. Not wanting him to think that she was nosy, S.B. quickly turned around and headed back toward Brenda's.

She hadn't gone far when a small red truck came up behind her. The driver slowed down and motioned for her to get in. It was Brenda.

"So, you decided to take a tour of the neighborhood," said the Pumpkin, as she shifted gears and pulled back onto the road.

"I heard the chain saws," said S.B. "I wanted to see where the sound was coming from."

"Looks like Harry Armstrong is clearing out some trees. I'm afraid Old Ogden Peleg isn't going to like that much," said Brenda. "That's his place back in the woods there." She pointed to the dented mailbox near the corner.

"Why would he care?" asked S.B. "They're just trees."

"They're not *just* trees to Old Ogden. He likes his privacy." Brenda swung the truck onto Turkey Hill Road. "He was born on that land and has lived there all his life. He has his house nestled in those woods, and he doesn't want anybody bothering him. Old Ogden keeps to himself."

"Is Harry Armstrong the professor who Finis does jobs for?"

"That's His Highness himself," said Brenda as she parked the truck between the two wood-stack walls of the carport. "You can help me get these groceries into the house, S.B."

S.B. took a bag of potatoes and a half gallon of milk and followed Brenda inside. "Don't you like Dr. Armstrong?" she asked.

"Not particularly. He thinks everyone should be as impressed with him as he is with himself," said Brenda, as she put the grocery bags on the kitchen table. "But he's been nice to Finis, so I probably shouldn't be so critical. By the way, is Finis home yet?"

S.B. shook her head. "When is he supposed to be back?" she asked, hoping that he might be in big trouble with Brenda. It would serve him right.

"By dark." Brenda began unloading the bags. "Sounds like you two didn't get along any better today."

"Not really. But it doesn't matter."

"Of course it matters," said Brenda. "It's nothing personal with you, though. Finis takes a while to warm up to people." Her frowning creases replaced the smiling ones. "You know, S.B., your dad and I had hoped that you'd have violin camp to entertain you. I don't know what we can do about that at this point."

"You don't have to do anything. I don't need anyone to do anything," said S.B. *Except to get me out of here!*

"Finis is used to being alone," continued Brenda. "He has always been independent."

And I'm not, thought S.B. That's what she means. Just wait until Brenda sees who the responsible and independent one is. "Finis didn't type those cards the way you told him to," she said.

"Darn that boy!" said Brenda. "I rushed to get home so I could deliver the baskets around dinnertime. There's a better chance of catching people home then."

S.B. went to the dining room to get the cards. "Don't worry, Brenda. I did the job for you." She handed the cards to her cousin.

"You sweetie!" Brenda looked at a card, then wrapped her arms around S.B., lifting her off the floor and kissing her cheek. "The sketch of the firecracker is the perfect touch. You have a knack for this business, S.B."

S.B. resisted the urge to wipe her hand across the moist spot on her cheek. She was pleased that Brenda liked what she had done.

"Just for that," said Brenda, "you can help me do my deliveries tonight. If you want to, that is."

"Sure," said S.B. She didn't have anything better to do. And it meant getting closer to civilization.

Together they loaded the Fourth of July baskets into the back of the truck. While S.B. struggled to fit the gorilla costume into the front, Brenda pulled a plastic bag from one of the garbage cans in the carport and tossed it into the back.

"It's a little cramped with the three of us," said Brenda as she squeezed into the driver's seat. "You need to lose a few pounds, Tarzan."

With everything ready, they drove toward town. Between Brenda's bulk and Tarzan's fuzz, the space left for S.B. was the size of a roach motel. She pressed against the door. The gorilla's itchy fur arm tumbled on top of her whenever the truck took a sharp turn.

"One of the deliveries is close to the Peking Lantern," said Brenda. "Do you like Chinese food, S.B.?"

"It's okay, I guess," S.B. mumbled as she picked fur from her mouth.

"Of course, that's slow, even for takeout, and we have to hustle our bustles if we're going to finish our deliveries by dark."

They turned onto a larger road, and S.B. noticed more houses and cars and even an occasional business. "Papa Tony's isn't too far out of our way," said Brenda. "But there again, pizza takes fifteen minutes, minimum."

"Whatever you choose is fine," said S.B. It was nearly six o'clock and her stomach was growling.

"That reminds me of a fantastic dish of lasagna I had in the Grand Tetons years ago," said Brenda. "Who would have expected good Italian food in Wyoming? But that can't compare with what you can get up in Syracuse. Large Italian population there. I know a restaurant owner who makes his sauce from tomatoes he grows on his roof." Brenda reached for the list of addresses on the dashboard. "Here's our first stop. I'll be right back."

And on it went, as they made deliveries at houses and apartments. At each stop, S.B. pulled the basket and balloons from the truck and handed them to Brenda to take to the front door. Between stops, Brenda talked about the food she'd eaten in her travels. The catfish in New Orleans. The sourdough bread in San Francisco. The lobster in Bangor. S.B.'s stomach roared louder with each new city.

"We did pretty well, kiddo," said Brenda, patting S.B.'s knee. "All but one customer home, and I'll catch him tomorrow afternoon before we go to the Fourth of July cookout at my boss's house."

"But there's another name on your list," said S.B.

"A Boo. We'll do that one on the way home," replied Brenda, as they turned into the parking lot of a steakhouse. "They have a wonderful salad bar here—soups, breads, sundaes with every topping you can imagine. And I have a half-price coupon for two rib eyes."

By the time they finished dinner, the street-
lights were on and darkness was closing in.
Brenda used the pay phone in front of the restaurant to call Finis. Assured that he was home, she
went into the ladies' room and slipped into the
gorilla costume.

"At least it cooled off outside," she said, as she
wedged herself in behind the truck's steering
wheel. "It's about thirty degrees hotter inside this
getup."

"Thanks for dinner," said S.B., remembering
her manners.

"Finis will be sorry he missed it." Brenda patted her stomach.

S.B. gazed out the window as they drove
through the streets of town. Her father's description had been a gross exaggeration. The "city" was
so small that they were on deserted country roads
in less than ten minutes.

"You haven't told me how you liked Cally,"
said Brenda.

"She was okay, I guess," said S.B.

"I'm surprised that she took off with Finis and
left you alone," said Brenda. "That's not like
Cally."

"She wanted me to come. I just didn't want to
go." S.B. looked across the seat at her cousin.
"She's kind of strange, you know."

"Strange?" asked Brenda.

"This morning when she came to the house, she knew you wanted me to meet her. But she claimed that you hadn't talked to her about me. Is that true?"

Brenda nodded.

"Then how did she know we'd been talking about her?" said S.B.

"Cally is extremely perceptive," said Brenda. "It's one of the things that make her a special sort of person."

"What do you mean?"

"She can really zero in on people," said Brenda, as she turned at an intersection. "She can see into a person and understand what makes him tick. It's a sixth sense."

"I think it's strange," muttered S.B.

Brenda smiled. "Depends on how you look at it."

S.B. hated it when adults said cryptic things like that. She slid closer to the door and stared out the window. Who cared, anyway? In twenty-five days she'd be gone from this place and these people, and it wouldn't matter.

Brenda jerked her head over her shoulder. "Oops, I just passed the place." She shifted into reverse and backed up in front of a small white house. "How about getting me that plastic bag in the back while I put on Tarzan's head?"

"What's in this?" asked S.B., as she pulled out the bag. "It smells awful."

Brenda laughed. "That's the idea. I've been saving up since I got the order last week. Fish heads, grapefruit rinds, coffee grounds, apple cores. You name it, it's in there."

S.B. wondered if her father and grandmother knew that Brenda drove around delivering garbage.

"A guy named Walter wanted me to dump this on the hall rug and say, 'This is for the garbage you've given me all these years,'" continued Brenda. "But I told him I only dump something like this outside. I can't risk getting sued for ruining someone's carpet."

"Why would he want to send a bag of garbage?"

"Oh, he's probably mad about a messy divorce or a raise he didn't get." Brenda adjusted Tarzan's head. "You'd better stay in the truck, S.B. Some people have no sense of humor."

S.B. rolled up her window and scrunched down in her seat. Brenda/Tarzan rang the doorbell. The door opened and Brenda disappeared inside the house. A few minutes later she lumbered back to the car with Tarzan's head in one hand and the bag of garbage in the other.

S.B. rolled down her window. "What happened?"

"Get me that last basket, S.B.," said Brenda, as she tossed the garbage bag into the back of the truck.

"But you were going to deliver it tomorrow."

"I'll make another." It was the first time that S.B. had heard her cousin sound angry.

S.B. pulled out the last balloon-and-lollipop basket. Brenda grabbed it and hurried back to the house. She was inside a long time. When she climbed back into the truck, her smile creases had returned.

"I have my standards," she said. "Nothing illegal and nothing cruel. That"—she gestured with her thumb toward the white house—"that was cruel. How could I dump wet coffee grounds at the feet of a dying old woman?"

"A dying woman?" S.B.'s eyes widened.

"Well, maybe not quite dying," said Brenda. "But she wasn't in good shape, I'll tell you that. It was Walter's mother. Can you believe it, S.B.?"

"Maybe she was mean to him."

"Foo." Brenda shook her head. "I'm a good judge of people. She didn't deserve that. I've half a mind to take this bag of garbage over to Walter's and dump it all on his head."

"So you changed the order?" asked S.B.

"You bet your booties I did. And it was worth it. The old girl loved the basket, especially the lollipops." Brenda smiled. "I told her the basket was from Walter. She loved that the best."

S.B. looked at her cousin wedged behind the steering wheel. Brenda wasn't like a pumpkin, after all. With her hair all frizzed up from wearing Tarzan's head and with her body covered by the gorilla costume, Brenda was more like a kiwi fruit. Hairy and coarse on the outside. Sweet and soft on the inside. And not at all an ordinary, run-of-the-mill sort of fruit.

Evening of Fireworks and Fairy Tales

I T W A S T H E Fourth of July, and the disease of the day was influenza.

That afternoon S.B. was minding her own business, trying to write poems for Boos and Balloons, when Finis barged in and sat down across from her at the kitchen table.

"Influenza is one of the deadliest diseases known to mankind," he announced.

"Everybody's had the flu," replied S.B. "So what?"

"The Spanish influenza of 1918 was not your garden-variety flu, S.B.," he said as he rocked on the chair's back legs. "Two billion people caught it. Millions died. Twenty-two million in ten months, to be exact."

"Big deal," she replied, without looking up from her tablet.

"More people died in one year from the Spanish flu than in four years of the Black Death during the fourteenth century." He leaned across the table. "You remember that one, don't you? The black swellings as big as—"

"I remember," said S.B. quickly.

"More Americans died from it than were killed in any U.S. war," he went on. "The bodies were stacked up because they couldn't bury them fast enough. The undertakers made a real killing." He laughed. "Get it?"

"I get it." S.B. made a face at him. "Don't you ever read sports books?"

"Not my style," he said. He shot a rubber band across the table. It missed her shoulder by an inch. "Dr. Armstrong's grandfather had it. He was a soldier in an army camp in Massachusetts. He almost died."

"Lucky for Dr. Armstrong that he didn't," said S.B.

"Lucky for the brain collection, too."

"The brain collection?" She hadn't meant to sound interested.

"Dr. Armstrong's grandfather's," said Finis. "It's the largest in the world. He collected seven hundred brains."

"Whose brains?"

"All sorts of people's. Some famous. Some not. He picked people with unusual habits."

"That's disgusting." S.B. wrinkled her nose. "Why did he do something like that?"

"To see if the folds in the brain have anything to do with personality."

"Sounds to me like Dr. Armstrong's grandfather's brain might have had a few kinks in it, too," muttered S.B.

Finis laughed. "Kinks. That's a good one, S.B." He reached over and pulled the tablet from under her hand.

"Give it back." She grabbed for it, but Finis held it out of her grasp.

"Let's see how good you are at writing these things," he said as he examined her work.

You're the best. You can't be beat.
So please enjoy these tasty treats.
That I'm wild about you is no fluke,
Because you're sweet and very cute,
Charming and handsome, that's for sure.
Love, your secret admirer.

Finis grabbed his throat with both hands and made gagging noises. "Who would send a dumb poem like that?"

"It's for a girl to send a guy she secretly likes."

"Very superficial, S.B."

"I don't care about your opinion," she replied. "Brenda says that kind of message is popular with the high school and college kids."

"I hate the word 'cute,' " said Finis.

"That's because no one ever called you that or ever will." S.B. finally got her hand on the tablet and snatched it away. "Could you leave me alone? I'm trying to concentrate."

"No problem. My ride will be here in a few minutes. I've got a *sparkling* Fourth of July planned this evening."

"Aren't you *punny* today?" murmured S.B.

Finis settled back in his chair. "So, what's the S.B. for? Brenda won't tell me."

"I thought you were going to leave me alone."

"Can I help it if I'm curious?" he said. "Besides, it must be something really awful for you to use the initials."

"You have a lot of nerve, criticizing anyone else's name, Minus Finis," said S.B. "What sort of name is yours, anyway?"

"A name of great significance," he said. "You know—Grand Finale. No more to follow. Save the best for last. It fits me perfectly, don't you think?" He shot another rubber band. This one grazed S.B.'s elbow. "How about Spoiled Brat? That would fit *you* perfectly."

S.B. tried her intimidating stare. Finis ignored it.

"Stolen Base?" he continued. "Maybe your parents were baseball fans."

"Do yourself a favor and forget it," said S.B. "If I wanted anyone to know my real name, I'd use it."

"It may take time," said Finis, "but I'll figure it out."

S.B. could imagine the mean jokes that Finis would make if he ever did figure it out. She hoped that he wasn't smart enough. Nobody in her school—despite many attempts—had ever guessed.

The gravel in the driveway crunched and a car horn blew. Brenda appeared from the front part of the house. "Sounds like Peter's here, Finis. Do you have all your stuff for the night?"

"Yeah, yeah." He gathered up his sleeping bag. On his way out the door, he kissed Brenda on the cheek. It surprised S.B. The Gruesome Trivia King didn't seem like the affectionate type. She wondered if living with the Kiwi did that to a person.

"See you tomorrow," said Brenda, waving once more before she went upstairs.

S.B. picked up her finished poem and followed her cousin. She found her sitting on the window seat in her bedroom, holding a hand mirror and starting to yank hair from her scalp with tweezers.

The sight made S.B. cringe. "What are you doing?" she asked."

"Beauty treatment," replied Brenda. "Can't let the gray hair ruin my image."

"Grammy says that two grow back for every one you pull," said S.B.

"If that happens, I'll have to pluck faster." Brenda tilted her head to the side. "Are there any in the back?"

S.B. leaned over Brenda's head. She spotted a half dozen long gray hairs but was afraid Brenda might ask her to pull them out. "None back here," she said.

Brenda sighed. "Good. I finally have them under control again."

"Why don't you just dye your hair?" asked S.B.

"Oh, I'm too young for that," said Brenda.

Too young? Didn't the Kiwi know that people with smile creases and gray hair weren't young anymore?

Brenda pushed herself off the window seat. "I'm glad Peter invited Finis to spend the night. Since we live so far out of town, he doesn't get to see his school friends often enough during the summer."

Too bad it wasn't for a week, thought S.B. Or better yet, four weeks. "Here." She handed her poem to Brenda. "It's not that good."

Brenda took a moment to read it. "Why, it's very, very good, S.B.," she said. "I like your poem, and so will the customers."

S.B. couldn't believe it. She'd created something Brenda could use for her business. This was better than a gold medal in typing. "I didn't think I could write well enough."

"You probably never tried," said Brenda. "I'll put this in my file. Business picks up when the college crowd comes back in September. This will be a big help then." She reached for her wallet on the dresser and handed S.B. five dollars.

"What's this for?" asked S.B.

"For typing the cards yesterday and writing this today," replied Brenda.

"But I liked doing it."

"If you work for Boos and Balloons, you get paid—even if it was fun." The Kiwi smiled. "I was right about you, S.B. There's something of your mother in you, more than the looks. Now, your father"—she chuckled—"your father would have asked for ten dollars and the copyright."

S.B. stuffed the bills into her shorts. Brenda's comment had ruined her happy mood. "That's the second time you've mentioned my mother," she said. "Why do you keep doing it?"

"Does it bother you?" asked Brenda, as she laid her mirror and tweezers on the dresser.

"I don't like you comparing me to her."

"S.B., your mother was creative, fun to be with, and a good friend. And like I told you, I'm a darned good judge of people, if I do say so myself." Brenda reached over and took S.B.'s hand. "So, you see, it's a compliment to you."

S.B. felt as if Brenda were tricking her into eating boiled squash by telling her it was orange sherbet. She would not be fooled. She knew what her mother had *really* been like. Grammy had told her.

"I'm going outside," she said, hurrying from the room before Brenda could say more.

When she got downstairs, she found company on the porch. Cally, wearing her faded yellow shirt and paint-spattered hat, sat in the wicker rocker, staring out at the glass ball. The porch floorboards creaked beneath her. The sound was like S.B.'s violin—squeaky and out of tune.

"Finis went to his friend's house for the night," said S.B., closing the screen behind her.

"I know." Cally looked over her shoulder at S.B. but didn't interrupt the steady rocking rhythm. "I came to see you."

"Oh." If this girl was trying to be friends, S.B. had news for her. No way was *that* going to happen. Cally wasn't like anyone she had ever met. There was something peculiar about her, and it wasn't just her appearance.

Neither girl spoke. The rocking and creaking filled the silence.

"The best place to see the fireworks tonight is on top of the hill," said Cally. "Come watch with me."

"What a super idea!" Brenda stepped onto the porch.

Cally jumped from the rocker and threw her arms around Brenda's waist—at least as far around as she could reach.

"You need some meat on those bones, kiddo," Brenda said as she returned Cally's hug. For a moment Cally's head disappeared beneath Brenda's flabby arms. "Why don't you go with her, S.B.?"

"I thought we were invited to a cookout at your boss's later this afternoon," said S.B.

"That would be less than exciting for you," said Brenda. "A bunch of dull adults gabbing about dull adult things. Going with Cally will be more fun, I'm sure."

S.B. felt trapped. Going to the cookout probably would be dull. But she didn't think she could tolerate an evening with Cally. Nothing about the girl was predictable, and S.B. liked to know what to expect—even if it was boring. While she stood there deciding what to do, Cally and Brenda made the decision for her.

"It'll be chilly. I'll find you a sweatshirt." Brenda hurried back into the house.

"We'll have our own picnic." Cally took S.B.'s hand and pulled her down the porch steps.

Brenda tossed S.B. a gray sweatshirt—one of Finis's. As it fell about her face, S.B. smelled the same pine scent that her sheets had from drying among the evergreen trees. She stuck the sweatshirt under her arm and let Cally lead her across the grass. There seemed to be no way to get out of going.

With Brenda waving from the porch, the two girls set off up the dusty road to the top of Turkey Hill. By the time they reached the twisted, poison ivy–covered tree that marked the path to Finis's swimming stream, S.B. was so winded that she had to stop. Cally waited for her.

"You get used to the hill," she said. "After a while a person can get used to anything. By the end of the month you'll be running up the hill."

"I doubt that," said S.B., as she tried to catch her breath.

As they walked farther, the road narrowed and the trees closed in above their heads, cutting out the sunlight. The air felt cool and smelled damp. But as they came around a curve in the road, they were blinded by the dazzling brightness of an open field.

"I didn't expect that," said S.B., shading her eyes against the sun's glare.

"Come on." Cally jumped over a low stone wall that bordered the dirt road. Holding her arms out as if they were wings, she ran into the field of tall grasses and wildflowers.

Thankful that she didn't have to go into the woods, S.B. took a deep breath and plunged in after Cally. The weeds were as high as her waist and scratched at her arms. She raised her arms high, just as Cally had.

She caught up to Cally in the middle of the meadow. The white-haired girl sat on a large flat boulder that jutted from the sea of wildflowers and grasses like an island. S.B. climbed onto the rock beside Cally and looked at the view. She felt as if she were on the top of the Empire State Building and could see four different states.

Cally pointed to a blue strip visible above the tops of the trees. "They'll shoot the fireworks over the lake. I've watched from here ever since I can remember."

"Will your family come out and watch with us?" asked S.B.

"One year it started to rain," said Cally, ignoring the question. "Everyone else went back, but I stayed." She lay back on the rock. "What do you see in those clouds, S.B.?"

"They're white. That doesn't mean rain, does it?"

"No, no. What do you *see*?"

S.B. squinted. No airplanes. No birds. No helicopters. "Nothing. What should I see?"

"Elephants. And there's a dragon shooting fire. And a fleet of tall ships."

"Oh, that," said S.B., vaguely remembering some long-ago time when she had played this game with someone. Someone who smelled like roses and held her close. A woman, not Grammy. Could it have been her mother?

"You can always tell when a storm is coming," Cally said, still staring at the sky. "It never sneaks up on you. There's always some warning, even though you might be too busy to notice. Dark clouds, faraway thunder, a change in the wind. People don't pay enough attention to the signs."

"I guess you're right," said S.B., still feeling uneasy with the memory.

"Let's make daisy chains," Cally said suddenly as she jumped off the rock. "Have you ever made one?"

S.B. shook her head.

"Help me gather flowers, and I'll show you how," said Cally, breaking off stems of white daisies and pink clovers.

Within a few minutes, the girls had collected two armfuls of flowers. They spread the blooms out on the rock between them.

"It's like braiding hair," said Cally, holding several stems in her hands. "You keep joining them together until you make a necklace."

S.B. watched as Cally worked, and soon she got the hang of it herself. After a while, each girl wore a wreath of white and pink flowers around her neck.

"It's getting late and I'm getting hungry," said Cally, draping her necklace over S.B.'s head. "I'll go get our dinner."

"Aren't we going to your house to eat?" asked S.B.

"I'll be back in a few minutes." Cally hopped from the rock and began running across the meadow.

"Can't I help?" S.B. shouted after her.

"I want to surprise you," Cally called back. "You stay there."

S.B. watched the white-haired girl sail through the weeds with outstretched arms until she disappeared behind the trees. Then, fluffing Finis's sweatshirt into a pillow, S.B. lay down on the rock and closed her eyes.

She was startled when Cally returned. "I didn't hear you coming across the field," said S.B., reaching down for the paper grocery bag that Cally carried.

"You must have fallen asleep," replied Cally. "It's a good place for a nap."

S.B. watched her spread their picnic dinner on the rock. It wasn't exactly her idea of a traditional Fourth of July meal. No hot dogs, burgers, chips, or soda. "Are you vegetarian or something?" she asked.

"I grew it all in my garden," replied Cally. "Even the tomatoes, and it's early for them."

Although the food wasn't what S.B. was used to, it was delicious. She was so full of raw peas, lettuce, broccoli florets, and spinach that she hardly had room for the oversized raisin cookies that Cally pulled from the bottom of the grocery bag.

"You must have a green thumb," said S.B. "I never knew veggies could taste so good."

"It's because they're picked fresh," replied Cally. "It's the taste of the earth in them."

They sat on the rock munching their cookies and watching the sun set over the lake. "Will your parents watch the fireworks with us?" asked S.B. She wondered why Cally hadn't taken her to her house and why there had been no sign of the family.

"I'm not sure," said Cally, gathering the remains of the meal into the grocery bag. "Is your father nice? Is he like Brenda?"

"Sure, he's nice," said S.B. "But he isn't like Brenda. Not at all."

"Does he take you places?"

"Of course," said S.B. "Anytime or anywhere I want." Except when he's working. Except when he's traveling. Except when he's out with friends. But no reason to mention that to Cally.

"You're lucky to have a nice father."

S.B. hoped that Cally would stop talking about her family. She was sure to ask about her mother. No matter which answer S.B. gave ("My parents got divorced" or "There was this plane crash"), people always asked more questions or gave their condolences or did something else to make S.B. feel awkward.

The white-haired girl touched S.B.'s arm. "It's better to think about what you have than what you've lost."

S.B. was unnerved. It was almost as if Cally had known what she was thinking. Was this the sixth sense that Brenda had referred to?

"People used to believe that goddesses spun a thread of life for every person at his birth," said Cally, as she tucked her legs beneath her.

"I never heard that," said S.B., thankful that Cally hadn't pursued the conversation about her parents.

"If your thread was gray and coarse, you would have a hard life," Cally continued. "If it was a fine thread of bright color, you had good fortune. If it was gold, you'd be a hero or a prince." She paused and looked at S.B. "Do you believe that?"

"It's just a fairy tale," said S.B.

"But do you think it's all decided right in the beginning like that?"

"I don't know if it is or not," she said. "I never thought about it."

"I hope it isn't," said Cally. She gazed across the field. "I really hope it isn't. Because I think my thread might be gray. But I keep feeling that it should be gold . . . that it's gold underneath, but the brightness can't show through. And if only I could rub off the gray, I could see the gold. Do you know what I mean?"

"Sort of," said S.B. "Like, if you could change a few things, your life would be a lot better."

Nodding, Cally smiled. "I like you, S.B."

It sounded weird to S.B. to hear someone say that. Kids at her school didn't walk around telling people they liked them. But at the same time, the comment pleased her.

They sat in the twilight, not talking. The air was full of cricket sounds and the whisper of wind through the trees at the edge of the meadow. Cally took off her hat and stuck it in her waistband. In the dimming light, S.B. thought that her wispy hair looked like white dandelion fluff about to float away.

The girl reached into the pocket of her purple shorts. Onto S.B.'s palm she dropped a small pebble. It was pink with flecks of shiny white.

"It's my amulet," she said.

If Cally hadn't looked so serious, S.B. would have laughed. "It's very nice," she said.

"Wrap your fingers around it," said Cally.

S.B. shook her head and tried to give the stone back.

"Try it. Just this once. I won't ask you again."

She shrugged. "Okay." She was Cally's dinner guest. It was the least she could do.

"Close your eyes," said Cally.

Not sure what to expect, S.B. closed her eyes and formed a fist around the pebble.

"There is a kingdom far away, and yet not so far," Cally began. "It is the kingdom of the Raging River and the Wild Wood and the Tangled Jungle and the Gorge of Death. In this kingdom there is treasure and treachery, kindness and cruelty, force and frailty, might and meekness. And in this kingdom dwell three, named Earth, Water, and Air."

S.B. had heard this before. Cally was telling the story from the glass ball. S.B. almost opened her eyes and said that she wasn't interested, but something in Cally's voice—softly speaking, almost singing—made her want to hear more.

"The task of the three—Earth, Water, Air— is to prevent cruelty from overcoming kindness, to keep the meek from being destroyed by the mighty," continued Cally. "They take their charge from the mysterious Lady of the Pines, whom they have never seen but who speaks to them through the Magic Sphere.

"Also dwelling in this kingdom is the Lord of the Green Realm, who uses his power to hinder them for reasons only he knows. Still," Cally went on, "there is balance, and respect for the riches of the kingdom by all who live there, including the Green Lord." She paused and lowered her voice to a whisper. "All except the Enchanter."

The breeze had become stronger and colder. It blew S.B.'s hair across her face. She shivered and clenched her fingers tighter around the pebble.

"The Enchanter is powerful and dangerous. He wants to destroy the perfect balance of the kingdom. His tools of destruction are deception and cunning. No one sees him for what he is, except the Lady of the Pines. She told Earth, who believed, and Water, who did not."

Suddenly there was a loud whistle and *pop-pop-pop*. S.B. opened her eyes. It was dark. A circle of colored sparks exploded in the black sky.

"The fireworks," said Cally.

The story was over, but S.B.'s heart still beat hard and fast. She felt excited and scared at the same time, as if she had just plunged off a high dive.

She watched the fireworks bursting over the lake and cheered with Cally as the night became bright with color. Each explosion was more spectacular than the one before, until the tremendous finale, when the entire sky above the lake was splattered with colored light.

And suddenly it ended. The sky was black, except for the fireflies blinking like Christmas lights. The only sounds S.B. heard were the cricket songs. Realizing that she still clutched Cally's pebble, she handed it to her.

"You felt it, didn't you?" said Cally, as she slipped the stone into her pocket. "You began to see the Story."

Had she? Was that what had happened? "It's getting cold," said S.B., as she pulled Finis's sweatshirt over her head. The smell of the pines was still on it. "I should get back."

They started across the meadow. Even though the moon was hidden behind the clouds, Cally moved as quickly as she had in daylight. S.B. stumbled behind her, unable to see more than a few feet ahead. As they came to the stone wall by the road, a man's voice broke the night's peacefulness.

"Cally!"

"Here, Pop," Cally called back. "Don't let him see you," she whispered as she scrambled over the wall. "I'll be back."

"When?" S.B. said, following her. But Cally had already disappeared into the darkness.

S.B. didn't like standing in the dark all alone. She kept thinking about the skunks, turkeys, and plague carriers. What if Cally didn't come back? She headed up the road after her.

A few yards ahead, she spotted lights behind the trees. As she came closer, S.B. saw a run-down trailer no larger than a school bus, its gray metal siding partly ripped off. The light coming through the tiny windows looked like the yellow eyes of a wild animal.

S.B. watched as Cally ran into the yard, dodging the mounds of tires and pieces of machinery littered about. A heavyset man stood in the open doorway. He grabbed Cally by the shoulder and pulled her inside. A woman's angry voice seeped out from the windows into the night.

S.B. backed into the shadows and looked behind her at the road leading downhill through the woods to Brenda's. It was pitch black, blacker even than a movie theater. Cally wouldn't be back, she knew. It would be a long, dark walk home.

As she stared into the darkness, S.B. heard a rattle. A few moments later two headlights bobbed around the curve. She crouched down, afraid to be seen. But as the headlights came closer, she saw the familiar shape of Brenda's truck. Jumping up, she ran out into the road, waving her arms.

"I came to get you when I heard the fireworks

end," said Brenda, as S.B. climbed into the truck. "Were they good this year?"

"Yes," answered S.B. Her voice was shaky.

Brenda turned the truck around and headed down the hill. S.B. watched out the back window as the lights of Cally's trailer disappeared behind the trees.

"You okay?" asked Brenda, looking over at her. "Did you have enough to eat?"

Count on Brenda to think she was hungry instead of scared. "We ate in the field," said S.B., glancing down at the wilted flowers around her neck. "Cally didn't take me to her house."

"She probably doesn't want you to know about that part of her life," said Brenda.

S.B. understood how Cally felt. She didn't want anyone to know about her mother, either. She didn't even want to think about it herself. But why was it that the one thing she didn't want to remember was the hardest to forget?

8

Revenge

SATURDAY WAS cleaning day. S.B. found this out when a duet of groaning roars woke her at 7:37 A.M. It created a stereophonic effect: Brenda in the hallway outside her door with a vacuum sweeper, Finis in the yard outside her window with a lawn mower.

S.B. also discovered that she was expected to make the duet a trio. As she stumbled, bleary eyed, into the hall, the Kiwi tossed her a dust rag. Although S.B. liked her surroundings to be clean, she never had to *do* the cleaning. Things were different at Brenda's.

By the time S.B. had dusted her room and the

woodwork in the upstairs hallway, Brenda had a new job for her. "S.B., come clear off this floor so I can vacuum," she said, opening the door to Finis's room.

S.B., who had been waiting for the chance to check out Finis's private space, surveyed the room carefully while she picked up the clothes and books. The posters on the walls had environmental slogans like "Save the Whales" and "Love Your Mother (Earth)." Across the room from his bed—unmade, of course—was a bookcase made from cinder blocks and boards. The top shelf was covered with animal skulls.

"How can he sleep in the same room with these?" she said to Brenda.

"Don't ask me," replied the Kiwi. "I'm just thankful that he doesn't keep roadkill in my refrigerator."

"You mean dead animals? Yuk!"

"Snap up the shade, S.B. Let's get some sunlight in here."

As S.B. reached to raise the shade, she noticed a paperback called *Name Your Baby* on Finis's desk. A bookmark was stuck near the back. S.B. was sure that it marked the *S* names. He wouldn't find her name in an ordinary name book, but it made her uneasy that he wasn't giving up. If he ever thought of using a horticulture guide, she'd be in big trouble. His teasing would never end.

Heading back to her room, S.B. figured that her contribution to Cleaning Day was completed. Brenda had other ideas. "There's a broom in the kitchen," the Kiwi called over the roar of the vacuum. "You can use it to knock down the cobwebs from the porch ceiling."

This did not thrill S.B. Cobwebs were made by spiders, which weren't her favorite animals. But she had a feeling that that wouldn't matter to Brenda. She went in search of the broom. When she came out on the front porch, she saw Finis trimming the grass around the tacky red-polka-dotted lawn lady.

"If it were me," he said to her, "I'd leave those cobwebs there to catch the mosquitoes."

"This wasn't my idea, believe me," said S.B., as she cautiously poked the broom up into a corner.

"I have to admit that those big black spiders don't make very attractive wall decorations." He looked up at her with the devilish grin that S.B. had learned to beware of.

Her mind was suddenly filled with the vision of a thousand hairy spiders climbing all over her body. She resisted the urge to jerk down the broom and search her hair for the creatures.

"The thing is," continued Finis, as he clipped around the fat woman's wooden legs, "we need spiders. Without them, the world would be crawling with bugs."

"Spiders *are* bugs," said S.B., yanking down a cobweb. It stuck all over the broom. She hoped that Brenda didn't expect her to clean it off. She wasn't about to touch that stuff.

"To be accurate," said Finis, "spiders are arachnids, not bugs."

"I don't care about scientific classification. If it's crawling on me, I don't like it."

"You're all wrong about this, S.B.," he said. "Spiders keep the insect population under control. Did you know that one pair of fleas, which only live about nine months, can produce a quarter-million offspring?"

"Okay, okay," she said, as her entire body started to itch. "If you promise to stop talking about it, I'll knock down the webs without killing the spiders."

With a triumphant grin, Finis took his clippers and moved to the glass ball. S.B. realized that he enjoyed annoying her with his arsenal of gruesome facts. It was a victory for him every time she reacted with a shudder.

"Interestingly, female black widows eat the male after they mate," said Finis, as he decapitated a dandelion.

"Sounds like a good arrangement," muttered S.B., wondering how she could get even with him.

"Other kinds of spiders," continued Finis, "weave warning signals into their webs so that birds won't fly into them and tear them apart."

"Warnings come in many forms," said a voice.

It was Cally. S.B. hadn't heard her come up the driveway, but there she was, standing on the stone path next to the porch. The girl crossed the grass to the glass ball, where Finis was crouched. "Remember the warning, Water."

At that moment Brenda came around the side of the house carrying an empty laundry basket. "The wash is on the line, and I'm ready to run some errands," she said as she pulled off her earphones. "Anybody want to go downtown with me?"

"I'm going to Dr. Armstrong's," said Finis, as he stood up. "He's going away for a few days, and he wants me to clear up the leftover twigs and brush before he goes."

"Did he happen to mention why in the world he cut down all those beautiful oaks?" asked Brenda.

"He said that they blocked the sun from his solar panels," said Finis.

"He shouldn't have done it," said Cally.

Finis shrugged and slipped his lawn clippers into his back pocket.

"How about you, Cally?" said Brenda. "Would you like a ride to the library?"

"Yes. My books are almost due," she said.

S.B. noticed the bookbag slung over Cally's shoulder. How had she known to show up at that moment with her library books?

"Library sound good to you, S.B.?" asked Brenda.

It sounded better than cobweb sweeping. "I guess so," she replied.

"You can borrow my card and get yourself some reading material, if you'd like," Brenda added. "I'll get the truck keys."

As soon as Brenda had gone, Cally marched over to Finis, who was gathering up his lawn tools from the porch step. "Water, you should come with us," she said.

"I have other things to do." Finis turned his back to her.

"You must beware of the Enchanter," she continued. "He is evil. He is a deceiver."

"Cut it out, Cally. I don't feel like playing today." He brushed past her and went inside the house.

Cally frowned. "He doesn't believe about the Enchanter," she said to S.B. "I told you that he doesn't. And there's trouble coming, Air. I feel it."

"I don't know what you're talking about, Cally," said S.B.

"The Enchanter has attacked the Dryads."

"The Dryads?" asked S.B.

"The wood nymphs," she replied. "The Enchanter has destroyed their home. The Green Lord won't like that. He'll seek revenge. There will be trouble."

S.B. didn't know what to say. Fortunately, Brenda came out with the keys and shooed the girls into the truck.

The drive to town was more comfortable than S.B.'s previous trip with Brenda had been, mostly because Cally was smaller and less hairy than Tarzan the gorilla. S.B. didn't want to let Cally know that she had seen her trailer and the way her parents had treated her. But if Cally was aware that S.B. knew her secret, she showed no sign. While they drove, she babbled to Brenda about the fireworks and her vegetable garden.

Brenda dropped them off across the street from the library. As they crossed the sidewalk,

S.B. noticed three girls hanging out at the bottom of the library steps. When she and Cally passed, Cally greeted them.

None of the girls answered. Instead they stared. S.B. recognized the kind of stare it was, too. She had given it to a few people herself. There had been that new girl in school, for example. The one nobody talked to all year.

S.B. had never considered how the girl might have felt, having a group of kids staring at her and whispering comments to one another behind their hands. Now she felt it herself. And it felt as if she were standing in front of a panel of judges who were rating her body, her clothes, her hair.

She didn't even know these girls. Why should she care what they thought about her . . . or Cally? But she did.

"Do they go to your school?" she asked Cally when they reached the top of the library steps.

"Who?" Cally pulled open the glass door.

"Those girls back there. The ones who didn't answer when you said hello."

"Oh, them. Yes, they're in my school," she replied.

"Don't you mind how they snubbed you?"

"That's just their way. I don't care."

Was Cally completely unaffected by what other people thought of her? S.B. wished that she were like that. It would make life easier.

Two women came up the library steps behind the girls. "We'd better go in. We're blocking the door," said Cally. "I'll be in Fiction if you need me."

S.B. watched the white-haired girl disappear into the stacks. She couldn't decide what she thought of her. If she'd met Cally back home, she never would have considered spending time with her. Cally wasn't the sort of girl you could have a pajama party with, or talk about boys with, or write silly notes to. The only reason S.B. was bothering with her at all was because there weren't any other kids around . . . except Finis, and he didn't count.

And yet, she could tell that Cally genuinely liked her. And it wasn't because she had the right looks or wore certain clothes or had traveled a lot. That gave S.B. a good feeling.

Although Cally's imagination was a bit wild, there was nothing brain-dead about her. In fact, she seemed pretty smart. Maybe there was more to Cally than S.B. had first thought.

She wandered over to the computer terminal. To kill time while she waited for Cally, she searched through the listings to see what kinds of books the library had. One of the entries that came up was a book on natural disasters. It gave S.B. an idea.

She collected a list of call numbers from the computer, then went into the stacks to find the books. By the time Brenda returned to pick up the girls, S.B. was loaded with enough ammunition to get even with Minus Finis Hatcher once and for all. She was going to beat the King of Gruesome Trivia at his own game.

9

Raspberry Picking

A FEW MORNINGS later, while S.B. was reading one of the library books in her room, the house began to vibrate from the sounds of a blaring stereo. She stomped down to the living room and found Finis on the sofa, examining an album cover.

"Turn that down!" she yelled.

"Sorry, did I bother you?" He got up from the sofa and switched off the sound.

"You're incredibly inconsiderate," she said, pulling her bathrobe around her.

"Before you go back upstairs, you might like to hear this one," said Finis, removing the record from the album cover he'd been holding. He placed it on the turntable and turned the sound back on.

It took only a few seconds for S.B. to recognize the song. The sound of the female singer's voice made her head ache and her face burn red. Did Finis know? Was he baiting her, waiting to see her reaction? "Where did you get that?" she managed to say.

"It's Brenda's," he said. "I never bothered listening to it before. Have you ever heard it?"

S.B. stared at him. He knew. She was sure of that. She had to stay calm. She couldn't let him see how she felt.

Holding the album cover, Finis walked over to the stairs, where S.B. stood frozen, her cheeks on fire. "You look exactly like her, only a couple years younger," he said, pointing to the album-cover photograph of the teenager with long auburn braids.

Here it comes, thought S.B. She bit her lower lip. She wished that he would turn off the music. "How did you find out?"

"It wasn't too hard to figure," he said. "Right in the middle of Brenda's impressive collection of jazz and classical is this 1960s rock album by flower child Auricia Tribble. I figured it must be something special for Brenda to have it. She hates rock music."

"Please turn it off."

"What's wrong? Don't you like it?"

"No," said S.B. "I hate it."

"It doesn't fit my tastes, either." Finis walked back to the stereo and switched it off.

"Did . . . did Brenda tell you anything about her?" asked S.B.

She couldn't bear for him to know. Finis's parents hadn't wanted to leave him. They couldn't help that they died. But *her* mother—her mother had left on purpose. She'd made her choice over a year before the plane crash that killed her. She'd picked the audiences over her daughter. "Your mother missed the fans," Grammy had said. "It wasn't enough for her to have the adoration of a husband and baby. She preferred the cheers of fifty thousand strangers."

"Did she tell you anything?" S.B. repeated.

Finis shook his head. "Brenda is very tight with other people's secrets."

The way he said "secrets" made S.B. wonder if he had guessed the truth anyway.

"It's obvious from the way you play the violin that you didn't inherit Auricia's musical talent," he said.

"Very funny," she muttered.

"The big question is," he said as he slipped the record back into the album cover, "did Auricia the singing Tribble name you, or did your father?"

"Can't you forget about my name?"

"I told you that I'm relentless when I want to find out something."

S.B. started up the stairs.

"Because if it was your mother's idea," he called after her, "it could be a musical term like Soprano-Bass or Sebastian Bach. Or Stop Button."

S.B. closed the door to her room and blocked out his string of words. Even if he hadn't realized it yet, Finis was uncomfortably close to guessing her name. Now that he knew about her mother's connection to pop music, he might figure out that her name came from a Beatles song. Then again, even Finis might not imagine that a mother would deliberately curse her baby that way.

She wished that he had never found that record. She hoped that he wouldn't mention it again.

After she made her bed and got dressed, S.B. continued her preparations for Finis's next gruesome trivia attack. Now she had even more reason to get even with him. This was war. She dragged out the pile of library books and continued her search for weapons.

She had started the day before with great disasters, figuring that anyone who got a kick out of plagues would be absolutely bowled over by a good disaster or two. Now she plunged into the biology books and old science magazines. Whenever she came across a useful fact, she wrote it down.

To her surprise, S.B. found that the reading was interesting and fun. By lunch, she had collected an arsenal of information. The next time Finis blasted her with disgusting trivia, she'd be ready for him!

As she organized her papers, there was a knock on her bedroom door. "I don't want to hear any more of your wild guesses, Finis," she called.

"It's Cally."

Glad that Cally had come to see her, S.B. opened the door.

The scrawny girl stood in the hall holding a white plastic bucket. She wore jeans, a man's tattered long-sleeved shirt, and her baseball hat. "Want to go raspberry picking?" she asked.

"I've never picked raspberries before," said S.B.

"It's easy. But put on long pants and sleeves, so you don't get all scratched up." Cally sat down on the edge of S.B.'s bed.

S.B. went to her bureau and took out different clothes. She hesitated, feeling awkward about changing in front of Cally.

"I won't look," said Cally, as if reading S.B.'s mind.

S.B. quickly slipped off her shorts and put on jeans.

"Where's Finis?" said Cally, keeping her back to S.B.

"I'm not sure. I don't think he went to Dr. Armstrong's house, though, because he's away on a trip. Maybe Finis went somewhere on his bike."

"He shouldn't spend so much time with Dr. Armstrong," said Cally. "That man isn't a good influence on Finis."

"Why do you say that?" asked S.B.

"He cares more about why people die than why they live," said Cally.

"That's just his job," said S.B., snapping the top of her jeans. "That doesn't make him a bad influence."

"He makes Finis think that way, too."

"Finis does have a sick sense of humor," said S.B.

"Finis would be better off thinking about living things. His parents would want that." Cally stood up and walked toward the door. "Are you ready?"

"I guess so," said S.B., as she pulled on a sweatshirt. "Where do we find these berries?"

"In an old field on the other side of the stream," said Cally. "Old Ogden used to graze cows there, but he doesn't bother anymore. The berry bushes have taken over."

Cally led the way up the dirt road. When they came to the twisted tree, she headed into the woods. S.B. wished that the raspberries had grown where they could reach them without tramping through the woods. She didn't like being surrounded by thousands of plants and animals. She felt much better when, at last, open sky appeared through the branches.

"Careful. Don't get caught," said Cally, as she held down a strand of barbed wire with her sneakered foot. "The berries are on the other side of this hedgerow."

Once they'd made it over the wire fence, the two girls ran into the sunlight. The entire field was covered with thorny raspberry canes full of plump, deep purple berries.

Cally plucked a handful and popped them into her mouth. "Try them, S.B.," she said. "Pick only the shiny dark ones."

Avoiding the sharp prickers on the cane, S.B. reached for a berry. It squished between her fingers. Gently, she picked another. It slipped easily from the plant. The berry was sweeter than the supermarket version she was used to. It had the same quality that Cally's vegetables had—the taste of earth.

"Good, aren't they?" said Cally.

"Delicious." S.B. ate her way to Cally's side and helped her add raspberries to the bucket.

They moved around the field, eating as many raspberries as they collected. S.B. was glad that she had worn long sleeves and pants, because the canes grabbed at her from all sides. After an hour the girls had worked their way to the opposite end of the field, and their hands were stained purple.

"I'm hot," said Cally, wiping her forehead. "I know a good place where we can cool off."

Taking turns carrying the bucket, they crawled under another section of barbed wire and walked into the woods. Cally stopped beneath a tall hickory tree.

S.B. looked up. Resting between the out-stretched branches about ten feet off the ground was a wooden platform. Pieces of wood had been nailed to the thick tree trunk to make a ladder. "A tree house," she said. "Did you build it?"

Cally took the bucket of berries and climbed up. "It's a deer blind," she said. "Hunters put it here."

"What's a deer blind?" asked S.B. as she followed Cally up onto the platform.

"The hunter sits up here until a deer wanders by. Then he shoots it. The deer doesn't see him because it can't look up."

"That doesn't seem fair," said S.B.

Cally shrugged. "Nature's not fair. It gave man a big brain and deer a neck that won't bend back."

S.B. looked at the view from their perch. They were surrounded by thick woods on three sides. But on the fourth side she could see the stream at the bottom of a twenty-foot-deep gorge. Across the gorge was a sunny clearing. And at the far edge of the clearing was a ramshackle wooden structure surrounded by piles of boards.

"What's that building?" she said.

"Old Ogden's barn. See his house off to the side behind those bushes?"

As they watched, a man with white hair and beard emerged from the house. He wore dark overalls and a red shirt.

"That's Old Ogden," whispered Cally.

"He looks like a skinny Santa Claus," said S.B.

"Don't let him see you," warned Cally. "He doesn't like anyone around his place."

When the man reached the barn, he picked up

a crowbar and began prying boards off the building.

"What's he doing?" said S.B.

"It looks like he's tearing down his barn," replied Cally.

"But why?"

Cally frowned. "I wonder if this has anything to do with the trees."

"What trees?" asked S.B.

Cally pointed to the side of the clearing opposite the barn. "The trees that aren't there anymore."

"You mean the ones Dr. Armstrong cut down?"

"Yes. Those were old and wonderful trees."

"Let's go," said S.B. "I feel funny spying on him."

Cally nodded, and they climbed down from the deer blind. As they walked out of the woods into the raspberry field, Cally handed the bucket to S.B., then took something from her pocket. S.B. recognized it as the pink-and-white stone that Cally had shown her the night they watched the fireworks.

"My amulet," began Cally, "has the magic power to help me understand. It protects us from evil. And there *is* evil. It's coming from the Enchanter. I felt it when we were in the Wild Wood."

Hearing Cally slip into her story embarrassed S.B. Not that anybody could see them. But S.B. wasn't used to someone her age pretending the way Cally did . . . as if it were all real. Yet the story intrigued her. "What awful thing is the Enchanter going to do?" she asked, despite feeling self-conscious.

Cally strode through the raspberry canes toward the opposite hedgerow. "He has already begun his cruel destruction of the kingdom. He has plundered the homes of the Dryads and driven them away. The Lord of the Green Realm will try to stop him from doing more wicked deeds."

"How?" Curious about these characters, S.B. hurried after the white-haired girl. "How can the Green Lord stop him if the Enchanter is more powerful?"

"The Green Lord is clever," Cally continued. "He has found a weakness in the Enchanter."

"A weakness?" asked S.B.

"I am not sure what the Green Lord will do, but he is preparing for battle, that is certain. He has a plan. We have seen it, Air, you and I."

"We have?"

Cally looked into S.B.'s eyes. "Yes, Air. You saw it from the tower in the Wild Wood. Remember?"

S.B. glanced over her shoulder. The woods did look wild and dangerous. And it was true that she and Cally had climbed a tower and spied on the old man while he worked. "Yes," she murmured, beginning to understand what Earth was saying. "He is preparing."

"Now we must warn our partner Water. The Enchanter will try to use him against us," said Earth, as they approached the hedgerow.

"He will?" Air felt the tingle of excitement.

"Yes," said Earth, "and against the Lady of the Pines and the Green Lord and the entire kingdom."

"But Water might not believe us," said Air.

"We must show him the Green Lord's work. We must convince him that a battle approaches. We must make him believe that the Enchanter is evil. We must make Water understand that he belongs on the side of the Green Lord. We must do it, Air, you and I!"

"I will—"

Suddenly, a burst of flapping brown feathers exploded in their faces. S.B. screamed and fell backward onto the ground, dropping the bucket of raspberries at the edge of the hedgerow.

"It was only a wild turkey," said Cally, helping her up. "We scared it."

S.B. brushed off the seat of her pants. *"We* scared *it?"* she exclaimed as she watched the enormous bird fly into the woods.

"It's over now." Cally gently patted her back.

Yes, it is over, thought S.B. The spell was broken. The Story had stopped. She was S.B. again. But for a few moments she had been Air. She had felt the evil of the Enchanter and the strength of the Green Lord. She had lived the Story.

Cally had made it happen. With her words she had transformed S.B. into Air and led her into another world—a world more exciting than music lessons or after-school programs or day camps. That world had been there all along, but S.B. hadn't been able to see it.

For those few moments, that other world had been real.

10

Yonder in the Realm of the Green Lord

I NEED A Boo for a man who's suing his business partner," said Brenda a few days later, as they cleaned up from dinner. She lifted a pot from the soapy water, rinsed it under the faucet, and handed it to S.B.

It was S.B.'s night to dry. She didn't mind, because she liked listening to Brenda talk about her business, travels, and friends. She was also learning more about food than she'd thought there was to know. "I'll come up with one," she said as she wiped the pot.

"I knew I could count on you." Brenda nudged S.B. with her elbow.

The back door banged open, and Finis rushed in. "The wasps are building a nest in the carport again," he announced. "One almost got me."

"I'll knock it down later tonight, when it gets cooler." Brenda handed S.B. the roasting pan. "Finis is allergic to wasp stings. He swells up like the Goodyear blimp."

S.B. pictured the headline: "Beanpole Transforms Into Goodyear Blimp. World Stunned." She giggled.

"It's not funny," said Finis, as he sat down at the kitchen table and took a bunch of grapes from the fruit dish.

"Yes, it is," said S.B., still giggling.

"That reminds me of a story," said Brenda, as she wiped her wet hands on her apron. "When Jon and I were little, we lived in the same town. I'm older than your dad, S.B., by a couple years, and I was always getting him out of trouble."

"You were?" S.B. couldn't imagine her father needing to be rescued by the Kiwi.

"Oh, it's true," said Brenda. "He'd get himself in a jam. Then good old Cousin Brenda would come on her white Schwinn to save the day. One afternoon I was jumping rope with my friends on the school playground when, all of a sudden, I heard, 'Help! Help!'" Brenda imitated the cry in a high, squeaky voice, which made S.B. and Finis laugh.

"Was it my dad?" asked S.B.

"You bet your booties it was," said Brenda. "I followed the cries to a wooden fence next to the playground. On the other side was a garage. I thought to myself, Has that little Jonny gotten himself locked in this garage?

"Then I spotted him. He was huddled between the side of the garage and the fence. Swarming all around him were yellow jackets—scores of the little buggers everywhere. Turns out that your dad was playing back there with some older boys and they accidentally disturbed the nest. The other kids climbed the fence and left poor Jon. He was too short to get out without help."

"So *you* helped him?" said S.B.

"Natch," replied Brenda. "I smeared mud all over his stings and took him home. Your grammy was so thankful that she gave me the entire batch of brownies she'd baked that morning."

"And my dad didn't get any?" asked S.B.

"No, but he didn't feel much like eating anyway." She laughed. "Maybe that's why Jon's thin and I'm"—grinning, Brenda patted her hips—"not."

The phone rang and Brenda went into the dining room to answer it.

"Say, S.B.," said Finis, as soon as Brenda left the room, "did you hear about the woman who wrapped her dead mother in a sheet and hid her between two mattresses for fifteen years?"

"Is this some kind of riddle?"

"No. This is an absolutely true story," said Finis, popping a grape into his mouth. "When people asked about her mother, the woman said, 'Mummy's sleeping.'" He laughed. "Pretty funny, eh?"

"Give me a break," muttered S.B., as she put the last pot in the cupboard.

"By chance, do you know what garbage collectors call maggots? I remembered this when I took out the garbage. I knew you'd be interested."

"You were wrong," said S.B.

"They call them 'walking rice.' It's the perfect name."

"Perfectly disgusting." S.B. wrinkled her nose. "Are you going to keep this up?" *Because if you are,* she thought, *you're in for a little surprise.*

"I bet you didn't know that flies are the first insects to arrive on a corpse," continued Finis, getting up from the chair and standing next to S.B. "They're incredibly sensitive to decomposing tissue. Within a half hour of death you can find fly eggs on a carcass. When the maggots hatch, they have a feast. Yum, yum." He smacked his lips next to her ear.

S.B. looked him in the eye. "Speaking of senses, Minus Finis, did you know that rats and hamsters have a better sense of smell than dogs?"

He blinked. "Where did you hear that?"

"It's true," said S.B. "As for humans, whose senses are very poor compared to other animals', hearing and eyesight ability peak at age ten. Just think, we're past our prime already."

"If this is *your* peak, S.B., I'd be pretty depressed about the rest of my life, if I were you."

"I'm only reporting what scientists say," continued S.B. without flinching. "By the way, did you know that eighty-five percent of all scientists who ever lived are alive today? Scientific knowledge doubles every fifteen years."

"Double. That's nothing," said Finis, jumping up to sit on the counter. "Coming from New York City, you'll appreciate this. An average roach infestation—about 5,000 per house—can multiply to 531 trillion in a year if not treated. Think of that the next time you see a roach in your bedroom."

"Sharks have 3,000 teeth," retorted S.B. "Think of that the next time you go to the beach."

He smiled. "You're not bad at this. But I'm sure you're not aware that a frog species that lives in South America is so poisonous that the sweat from a single frog can kill 1,500 people." He folded his arms and looked down at her. "What do you have to say to that?"

S.B. could tell that he was enjoying himself. But he didn't realize that she could keep this up for a long time. She'd read a lot of books in the past week. "I happen to know that 900 million cards are exchanged every Valentine's Day."

"Then you won't notice if I don't send you one next year," said Finis.

"And," continued S.B., "I know that over 82 million Etch-a-Sketches have been sold since 1960, which is amazing for a toy that doesn't break."

"That's peanuts," said Finis. "How about this one? Americans use 18 billion disposable diapers a year. Check it out, S.B., 18 *billion!*"

S.B. didn't hesitate. "Antarctica contains ninety percent of the ice on Earth."

"Ice is boring. Hail, on the other hand, is interesting," said Finis. "In Ohio in 1981, hailstones weighing as much as 30 pounds killed 5 and injured 225."

"A storage tank in Boston burst in 1919 and two dozen people were smothered by molasses."

"Is that the best you can do?" He snickered. "Think major disaster, S.B. Think extraterrestrial. Like the meteor that hit Siberia in 1908 and destroyed all plant life for one thousand square miles. That's major!"

"All right. How about this, Mr. Gruesome Trivia King?" she said. "An earthquake in China in 1976 killed 242,000 people."

As S.B. waited for Finis's comeback, Brenda returned to the kitchen from the dining room. "Your father is calling from Paris, S.B.," she said.

S.B. had been having a wonderful time sparring with Finis. Brenda's words ruined everything. "I don't want to talk to him," she said.

"But you know he's been trying to get you for days and getting stuck with my answering machine," said Brenda. "He sounds like he misses you."

"I doubt it," muttered S.B.

"Go on, honey. Get the phone," Brenda urged.

It was hard to argue with the Kiwi. Dragging her feet, S.B. went into the dining room. Tarzan the gorilla stared at her. She stuck out her tongue at him while she picked up the phone. "Hi, Dad," she said. "What's new on the Continent?"

"Did you get any of my cards yet?" he asked, sounding annoyingly pleasant.

"Not yet," she replied. No slashing and burning of his "pretty postcards" had yet occurred . . . but it would.

"How do you like your summer so far?" he asked.

S.B. had no intention of mentioning that Brenda was a rather nice Kiwi fruit, or that Cally was sort of interesting and unusual company, or that battles with Finis were almost fun. "I haven't been swimming or sailing or waterskiing the way you promised," she said coldly. "And I haven't touched my violin at all." She knew he'd hate that!

"That's okay."

"What?" S.B. was shocked. "Didn't you hear me? I haven't practiced one teeny bit for almost two weeks."

"You're doing other things instead," said her father. "Brenda's been telling me how you've helped with her business. I'm glad to hear that you're trying new things."

"You don't get it, Daddy. Except for writing a few dumb poems, I'm doing absolutely nothing. My mind is wasting away. It's worse than watching TV all day."

"Brenda mentioned a trip to the library."

"That was nothing," said S.B. "You made a big mistake sending me here. It's been a totally unproductive summer. Worse than YMCA camp. Remember how you took me out of that because I wasn't learning anything?"

"It sounds to me as if you're learning plenty," he said. "In case I can't get you by phone again, I'll see you in a couple of weeks. I love you."

And the call ended. Without S.B. slamming down the receiver. Without S.B. convincing him that she was suffering and withering away. Without S.B. being able to shock and unnerve him even a little bit.

He wasn't upset. He wasn't surprised. He didn't even seem fooled by her complaints. It was as if he'd known all along what her summer would be like. It was almost as if—though S.B. couldn't imagine why her father would do this— he had planned it that way.

A letter from Grammy arrived in the next morning's mail. And, as S.B. expected, it included a five-dollar bill. It also included S.B.'s original letter with red marks showing a missing question mark and comma. She stuffed the money into her pocket and read what Grammy had to say about her cat, Ike, named after President Eisenhower.

As she rooted in the stack of mail for a post-card from her father—to rip up and burn, of course—Finis came out on the porch.

"Anything for me?" he asked as he sat down on the other wicker chair.

S.B. handed him the bundle of mail. "Nothing but magazines and bills," she said.

"Were you making up that trivia stuff last night?" he said.

"No," replied S.B. "It was all true."

"Well, some of it was mildly interesting." He glanced over at her. "You didn't turn out to be as much of a pain as I first thought you'd be."

"Thanks . . . I think."

"Southern Botswanaland?" he said.

"What?"

"I hadn't considered geographical locations for your name before," he said. "Am I on the right track?"

"You're way off," she said, glad that he'd given up on the music connection.

"How about Sow Bug? Or Soy Bean?"

She shook her head.

"Space Bar? You like to type."

"You're being ridiculous," she said.

"How about Rumplestiltskin?"

"What's that have to do with 'S.B.'?"

He laughed. "It worked in the fairy tale."

"Speaking of fairy tales," said S.B., "can I ask you something about Cally? It's about that story of hers."

Finis stopped rocking. "What about it?"

"How long have you been playing it with her?"

"Since I came to live with Brenda last summer," he replied. "The whole thing was her idea, but I got sucked in somehow."

Sucked in. It had happened to S.B., too. At first the Story had seemed like a movie that flickered across the television screen while S.B. concentrated on something else in a far corner of the room. Gradually, she was pulled closer and closer, until she found herself inside it. Cally had made her a part of it . . . a main character.

"I don't understand the names she's given us," said S.B. "What do they mean?"

"She told me that it has to do with the ancient elements," said Finis. "Cally reads a lot about myths. That's why she calls herself Earth. You know, Mother Earth and all that. I'm Water because I like to swim. And you're Air because you came here by airplane. It's her game, so she gets to do the naming." He stood up and looked down at S.B. "You probably think it's all very weird."

"Well, I did in the beginning," said S.B. "But now . . . Well, she makes it so convincing."

Staring across the grass toward the glass ball, Finis nodded. "Sometimes it can seem totally real," he said. "I feel like I'm a great adventurer named

Water who lives in a wild and dangerous kingdom. And other times it just seems like a complicated game that Cally made up."

"She acts like it's more than a game," said S.B.

"For her, I think it is," said Finis. "If I had to live the way she does—up there with parents like hers . . ." He shrugged. "Hey, I don't blame her for wanting to live in the Green Realm."

"Morning," called a voice.

They both looked toward the end of the driveway. It was Cally.

"We were just talking about you," Finis called back.

"And here I am."

S.B. leaned toward Finis and whispered, "Why'd you say that? I don't want her to know that we were discussing her behind her back."

"Cally wouldn't care," he said.

S.B. wanted to ask how he could be so sure, but Cally had crossed the lawn and stood below them, beside the glass ball.

"We have work to do," said the white-haired girl.

"What kind of work?" asked Finis.

"You need to see something," she replied.

"Coming, S.B.?" said Finis, as he jumped off the porch.

S.B. followed him across the grass. Although she still felt self-conscious playing Cally's game, her experience in the raspberry field had been like a brief, exciting visit to a new place. She was eager to return.

Cally pinched off a pink flower near the base of the pedestal and brushed it back and forth over the surface of the glass ball. "Magic Sphere, Magic Sphere, we are here." She laid the pink flower on top of the ball. "Magic Sphere, we are here," she repeated, her voice becoming deeper.

Then the three of them placed their hands on the glass ball. S.B. closed her eyes and let Cally's words sweep over her.

"The Lady of the Pines warned that this day would come. Our kingdom is in danger. We must do what we can to protect it. But we need to learn more. Today we will go to the Tangled Jungle on a spy mission."

They opened their eyes and drew their hands away from the Magic Sphere. Then the three— Earth, frail and small, with keen senses; Water, tall and strong, with quick feet and mind; Air, brave and adventuresome, with blazing hair and sharp eyes—crossed the Plain of Green and the Rocky Desert on their way to the Tangled Jungle.

Water led because he knew the shortest path. Earth came next, followed by Air. Because they were strong and clever, they made the journey at great speed and without detection by their enemies.

When they arrived at the Tangled Jungle, Air (who did not know the hidden trails as well as the other two) crawled under the Arch of Protection behind her companions. Standing upright on the other side, she looked above her head at the vines that had fused into a roof. The adventurers were completely hidden. Neither the Green Lord nor the Enchanter could find them there. The magic of the vines shielded them.

"Where are we going?" asked Air, as she followed Earth and Water through the dark and secret passageways of the Tangled Jungle.

"To the Gorge of Death," answered Earth, in her strong, clear voice. "It is just ahead. And yonder is the realm of the Green Lord."

Soon Air saw light. They had arrived at the Gorge of Death. On the other side was the Green Lord's castle.

"Below is the Raging River," said Water, pointing into the dark chasm. "But here we can cross the Gorge of Death safely. It is a mystical place, protected by the magic of the Tangled Jungle."

Water had great knowledge of the kingdom's waterways. Only at this one magical spot did the two earthen banks lean far out over the Raging River, as if reaching for each other.

"Do as we do, Air," said Earth. She patted Air's shoulder. "And you will know the secret of the crossing."

Air watched Water and Earth fly across the Gorge of Death. From the opposite side, they called the secret words to her, the words that would help her cross. The magic erased her fear. It gave her powers of flight. With one swift and graceful movement, she flew safely across to her companions.

They could see the Green Lord's castle from where they stood.

"He is tearing down his castle," said Earth. "The Dryads are helping him. See them pulling at the castle walls."

Water frowned. "What does this mean?" he asked.

"The Green Lord is preparing for battle," replied Earth. "The Enchanter has destroyed the Dryads' homes. The Green Lord will help the Dryads get their revenge. He must use the magic that is locked within the castle's walls to weaken the Enchanter's power."

"There is no Enchanter," said Water. "I have told you before. It is the Green Lord who is our enemy."

"The Enchanter changes form so you do not see his true spirit," said Earth. "He is evil. The Green Lord knows. The Lady of the Pines knows."

"I'm going home." Water jumped back across the Gorge of Death.

"No, you must not," called Earth, following him across. "We must help the Green Lord. It is our duty . . . our destiny."

"Not mine!" Water disappeared into the Tangled Jungle.

"Hurry, Air! Help me stop him!" yelled Earth over her shoulder, as she ran after him.

Air looked down into the depths of the Gorge of Death. She was afraid. Her companions had departed without telling her the secret of crossing back. But she had to follow. She could not let Water desert them. He was needed to help the Green Lord. Besides, she did not know the path back to the Magic Sphere.

She stepped away from the edge. Taking a deep breath, Air ran toward the Gorge. At the edge she jumped, using all her power to fly across the abyss. But as she landed on the soft, loose soil of the opposite bank, only inches from the safety of the Tangled Jungle, she slipped. Her powers could not prevent her from falling ... falling into the Gorge of Death.

11

Fence Building

WHEN S.B. OPENED her eyes, the old man was leaning over her leg, applying a bandage. She recognized him immediately. He wore the same dark overalls and red shirt.

"Good. You're all right, then," he said, stroking his white beard. "Things look blurry at all?"

She lay on the grass between a pile of splintery boards and Old Ogden's barn. Most of the barn's walls were gone, leaving only the stone foundation, the roof, and a wood frame skeleton. Squinting in the sunlight, she sat up and glanced across the grass toward the gorge. For a second, she thought she saw Cally peering out from a jumble of vines on the opposite side. "I can see okay," she said.

"Guess you just had the wind knocked out of you." Old Ogden looked across the gorge and shook his head. "I don't like you kids poking around here. You make too much noise. Bother the creatures. Trample the wildflowers. Get yourselves in trouble."

S.B. pushed herself up. "I'm sorry for bothering you. I'll go now."

"Better stay off them feet for a few minutes, until that leg stops bleeding," Old Ogden said as he bent to pick up an armful of boards from the pile next to her.

S.B. pulled back the bandage and examined the scrape on her leg. It didn't look too serious. But her clothes and skin were brown with mud. "How did I get up here from the stream?" she asked.

"I carried you," he said gruffly. "And I can't say it was the best thing for my back, neither."

S.B. watched him load the boards into a wheelbarrow. He moved quickly for someone so old. S.B. figured he must be strong, too, to have carried her. Remembering how she came to be there in the first place, she decided to find out what she could. Cally and Finis would be impressed if she came back with some information.

"Why are you tearing apart your barn?" she asked.

Old Ogden threw a board into the wheelbarrow. It landed with a crack. Turning, he stared at S.B. "Just look!"

The fierceness of his voice frightened her.

Wiping his hands on his overalls, Old Ogden strode to the opposite end of the clearing and motioned to a wooden box nailed to a tree. "See that, girl?"

"What is it?" asked S.B., as she got to her feet. She couldn't decide whether to run for her life or stay to hear the answer to her question.

"I put that up for my birds," he said. "Got a mother bluebird and five eggs in there right now. Sometimes chickadees come. Sometimes wrens." He pointed. "Now look at that, will you?"

S.B. took a few steps toward him. The old man was still far enough away that she could run if she had to. She looked where he pointed, but all she could see were tree stumps and several piles of brush. She recognized it as the area that Dr. Armstrong's men had cleared the previous week.

"All a man asks for is to be left alone." Old Ogden walked back toward her.

"I'm sorry for being on your property," said S.B. "We didn't think you'd mind." She hoped he wouldn't call Brenda and complain about her trespassing. Maybe he wouldn't realize that she was Brenda's cousin.

"Some people just can't leave things the way they belong," he continued as he grabbed a weathered gray board from the pile on the ground. "They've got to fool with things that ought not be fooled with."

"But we didn't touch anything," said S.B., looking behind her. The driveway out to the road had to be there somewhere. She wanted to get away before Old Ogden decided to call the police . . . or worse.

"Everything was fine until *he* came," said the old man, becoming more agitated. "If I'd known what he was up to, I wouldn't have sold him a single acre. The land has a history. Don't people know that anymore? Takes fifty years for one of them trees to grow that big. Only five minutes to slash it down. And for what?"

"I . . . I don't know," croaked S.B.

"He's not going to plant corn or wheat or nothing else. Oh no." Shaking his fist, Old Ogden stomped between the woodpile and his wheelbarrow. "He just wanted more sun on his windows. If he wanted sun, why did he build his fool house in the woods? Tell me that, girl!"

"I think I'd better go now," said S.B., backing away.

Squinting, Old Ogden stared at her.

"I'm feeling okay," she said. "Really."

"Well, don't let me catch you around here again," he said in a calmer voice.

"You won't." S.B. turned around. Then, remembering that the old man had, in fact, rescued her, she added, "Thanks for helping me out of the gorge."

"Don't make me have to do it again," he grumbled.

Brenda was loading baskets into her truck when S.B. got back to the house. She didn't look angry, so S.B. figured that Old Ogden hadn't called to complain—yet. "Where are Cally and Finis?" she asked the Kiwi.

"Haven't seen them," said Brenda.

Some friends they are, thought S.B. I could have been killed by the fall into the gorge. Or by Old Ogden. And they ran off and left me.

"What happened to your clothes and your knee?" asked Brenda, bending down to get a closer look.

"I tripped," said S.B., thinking it wise not to mention any details about the accident. "It's nothing serious."

"I have a few Boos and Balloons deliveries to make this afternoon," said Brenda. "How about helping me out when you get cleaned up?"

"Okay," said S.B., as she headed inside to change her clothes. Staying out of the way for a while might be a good idea. It would give Old Ogden time to simmer down.

After she helped her cousin load the rest of the baskets into the truck, they set off down the road. About halfway to town, Brenda pulled an envelope from her blouse pocket and handed it to S.B. "I want you to have these," she said.

S.B. stared at the white envelope. She could feel snapshots inside. She had a funny feeling about those snapshots. It was a trap—hidden in that clean white envelope. And she was going to walk right into it.

"Open it, S.B.," insisted Brenda.

Realizing that her cousin gave her no choice, S.B. slipped open the flap and pulled out the seven photos. Her suspicions had been right. *Snap*. The trap shut on her.

"They were taken at your parents' wedding," said Brenda, glancing across the seat at S.B. "Doesn't Jon look different with a beard? And your mother was gorgeous. You can't tell from the pictures, but her hair was nearly to her waist. She designed the dress herself."

"You're not supposed to wear a dress like that in a wedding," muttered S.B. "It looks silly."

"That's the way things were back then. People wanted to break with tradition," said Brenda. "You keep the pictures."

S.B. shook her head. "I don't want them. My dad wouldn't want me to take them."

"Yes, he would," said Brenda in her peachy voice. "Last night he asked me to give them to you."

"My father?" That sounded all wrong to S.B. "He hates to see her pictures. He threw them all away. Grammy told me."

"Your grammy told you part of the story," said Brenda. "The part she saw and believed was true. But there can be different ways to see the same picture, different angles to the same reality."

S.B. didn't see how there could be a different angle, a positive one, to her mother's story. Selfish. Addicted to fame. Irresponsible. That's what she'd been. Grammy said so.

"I met your mother in college," said Brenda, as she steered the truck onto a side street. "She was very talented—already a celebrity because of the albums that she'd recorded as a girl during the late sixties and early seventies. I introduced her to Jon and they hit it off immediately. They got married, you came along a few years later, and everything seemed perfect. The problem was—"

"I know the rest," interrupted S.B. "She gave me a stupid hippie name. Then she decided that she'd rather be a rock star than my mother, so she ran off. Now, could we stop talking about it?"

"That's the way some people might have seen it," said Brenda. "But it wasn't that simple."

"Oh sure," muttered S.B.

"She loved traveling and recording. And she'd been away from it since college—over ten years. It was frustrating for her to teach singing to others. What she really wanted was to perform again herself."

"I guess it was frustrating for her to be a mother, too, right?"

"Not at all," said Brenda. "That was the one part of her life that she was happy about. But when the chance came to restart her career—" She glanced at S.B. "I know that if she hadn't been killed in the plane crash, she would have come back to see you every chance she had."

"She wouldn't have been in that plane if she hadn't gone off on some singing tour," said S.B.

"She wanted you with her, S.B.," said Brenda. "But your father wouldn't let her take you. There was a nasty legal battle. Jon won, and it was the right decision. You were only two years old, and it wouldn't have been a good way for you to grow up. Your mother was forced to make a difficult choice. She missed you terribly."

"She didn't want to leave me?" asked S.B. It had never occurred to her that her mother might have missed her. "If that's true, why didn't my dad ever tell me? He never told me anything about her."

"He went through a lot of pain when your mother left, and more the next year when she was killed. It was hard for him to talk to you about her, especially when you were young." Brenda reached over and patted S.B.'s hand. "But you're old enough now to understand. He wants you to look at things from a different angle. That's one reason he sent you here."

"Because you knew my mother?"

"That, and because . . . Well, remember how I told you I used to come to your dad's rescue, astride my white Schwinn, when we were kids? Now I have a red Toyota, but I'm still there when he needs my help." She put her arm around S.B.'s shoulders. "You're growing up so fast, kiddo. It scared him a little."

S.B. shrugged.

"She wasn't the bad person you think, S.B.," said Brenda. "Maybe if you ask your dad more when you get home, that will make it easier for him to talk about her."

S.B. stuffed the snapshots back into the clean white envelope. "I'll think about it," she said. She hated being tricked.

There was no more said about the photos or S.B.'s parents. Brenda seemed to take the hint—at least temporarily—that S.B. wanted the subject dropped. S.B. found it hard to stay annoyed with the Kiwi. She liked her cousin too much, despite her occasional trickery. She tucked the envelope of photographs into her violin case, where they were out of sight, if not out of mind.

The next morning, S.B. overslept. Finis and Brenda were just finishing up their breakfast when she came downstairs.

"You both look like raccoons with those dark rings under your eyes," said Brenda.

"I really didn't sleep well last night," said S.B. "I guess that's why I had a hard time getting up this morning."

"Join the club," said Finis. "It sounded like someone was banging a drum all night. Didn't you hear it, Brenda?"

She shook her head. "You know me. My head hits the pillow and I'm out. Good as dead."

"I wonder what it was," said S.B.

"I don't know," said Finis, "but I'm glad it's over at last."

But, as they learned later in the day, it was far from over. Finis brought the news home that afternoon when he returned from mowing Dr. Armstrong's lawn.

"You have to see this, Brenda!" he cried as he burst into the kitchen, nearly knocking S.B. off her feet.

"Calm down," said Brenda. "See what?"

"Dr. Armstrong was gone all week, remember?"

"Yes," said Brenda. "So?"

"So he came home this morning, and guess what he found?"

"Besides tall grass?" said Brenda, smiling.

"This is serious," said Finis. "Come on. You have to see it."

He pestered her until Brenda agreed to go with him. Tingling with curiosity, S.B. ran behind Finis, down Turkey Hill and onto Skunk Hollow Road. Brenda, who was in no shape to keep up with them, ambled behind. After they passed Old Ogden's rusty mailbox, S.B. spotted someone standing on the shoulder of the road ahead. She recognized him as the man she had seen giving orders the day the trees were chain-sawed.

"Who does Ogden Peleg think he is?" shouted Armstrong.

He was tall and gaunt, with a sharp face and thinning gray hair. His eyes were dark and un-friendly. S.B. disliked him immediately. Going no closer, she waited for Brenda. Finis, however, ran to the man's side.

"What's the problem, Harvey?" asked Brenda, as she puffed her way toward them.

"Dr. Armstrong was gone for a few days," said Finis, "and look what Old Ogden did."

"See for yourself," said Armstrong, pointing toward his yard.

At the edge of the smooth carpet of freshly cut grass stood a rickety fence. It had been positioned next to the line of tree stumps and extended from the road to the woods behind Armstrong's house. The fence, which was over six feet tall, was built of old gray boards crudely hammered together. Since all the boards were different heights, the fence's top edge created a jagged line between the hacked-off stumps and the immaculate lawn.

As soon as she saw it, S.B. knew the fence had been made with the boards from Old Ogden's barn.

"I think Old Ogden is trying to tell you something, Harvey," said Brenda. S.B. caught sight of a smile twitching on her lips. "He must have put the whole thing up last night," continued the Kiwi. "Amazing."

"It's outrageous!" screamed Armstrong. "And he won't get away with it."

"I don't think there's much you can do about it, Harvey," said Brenda.

"There's plenty I can do, believe me." He shook a bony fist in the direction of the fence. "No one gets away with that. I won't tolerate it."

"I wouldn't overreact, if I were you," said Brenda, as she turned to leave. "Come on, kids. I've seen enough."

As the three of them walked back to the house, Finis glared at Brenda. "I bet it would be different if Old Ogden had built a fence like that next to your house," he said.

"I would never give Old Ogden a reason to do that to me," she replied.

Finis kicked at the dirt. "Are you saying that Dr. Armstrong asked for this?"

Brenda stopped walking. "I'm saying that Dr. Armstrong was asking for problems when he chain-sawed all those trees along Old Ogden's property. Now let's go home."

S.B. could tell that Finis was annoyed with Brenda. Brenda was disgusted with Armstrong. Armstrong was angry at Old Ogden. All this fuss over a silly fence! It was just a neighborhood disagreement. Nothing serious.

So why did she feel as if something awful were going to happen?

In Danger

"OLD OGDEN TORE down his barn to build a fence," S.B. told Cally the next afternoon. They were sitting on Brenda's porch playing Scrabble. "He built it right up against Dr. Armstrong's lawn, and it looks awful. Armstrong is really ticked off."

"Dr. Armstrong shouldn't have cut down the trees," said Cally.

"That's what Brenda says," continued S.B. "She says the trees might have belonged to Old Ogden in the first place, and Armstrong had no right to touch them."

"I knew trouble was brewing," said Cally. She

glanced toward the glass ball in the middle of the grass. "The battle has started."

The postman's car crunched up the dirt road and stopped at Brenda's mailbox. He waved as he continued up the hill to Cally's house.

"Let's see what came." Cally jumped off the porch and ran down the driveway. "I love mail. I don't usually get any, though."

"When I get back to New York, I'll write you," said S.B.

"Will you?" asked Cally, her eyes wide. "I'd like that." She pulled the letters from the mailbox.

"Mostly junk, I bet," said S.B.

"Look. A postcard for you," said Cally. "The Eiffel Tower. I've never seen a postmark from another country." She handed the card to S.B.

S.B. handed it back. "You can keep it if you want."

"Don't you even want to read it?"

"No." S.B. shook her head. "It's from my father. I'm not interested in anything he has to say."

"Why not?" Cally turned the card over and looked at the back.

"He tricked me into coming here so he could go to Europe without me."

"You don't like it here?"

"No offense," said S.B. "This isn't a bad place, really. It's just that I don't like the way he made me come."

"I guess my vegetable seedlings feel that way, too," said Cally, as they walked back to the porch.

"Your vegetables?" said S.B.

"I plant tomato seeds in the house early in the spring when it's still cold outside," said Cally. "But before I can plant the little seedlings out in the garden for the summer, I have to get them used to the hot sun and to not having as much water." She traced the outline of the Eiffel Tower with her fingers. "For a couple weeks I set them out in the sun, a little longer each day, and I gradually give them less water. It's called 'hardening off.' The seedlings couldn't survive very long in the garden if I didn't do it."

"What's that have to do with my father?" asked S.B.

"You have to harden off vegetables if you want them to grow healthy and strong," said Cally. "Maybe he had the same idea when he sent you to be with Brenda."

"My father doesn't know anything about gardening," muttered S.B.

But the conversation reminded her of something. As she took the mail into the house, S.B.

thought about the daffodils. She'd forgotten all about them until Cally mentioned her plants.

It had happened a few months before, when she and her father had gone to a mall to shop for her birthday. He always let her pick out new clothes as part of her present.

"I need to buy bras," S.B. had told him. She'd been surprised by the shocked look on his face.

"Are you sure?" he said. "But you're still so young."

"Eleven isn't young," she said. "Half the girls in my class have been wearing them since fall."

"I thought Grammy would help out on this," he murmured.

"I can't wait until we see Grammy again. I need them now. Come on." She took her father's hand. "They have them over in this store."

He opened his wallet and took out some money. "You go get what you need. I don't know that much about women's things. I'll wait out here for you."

When she came out of the store, S.B. was wearing one of her new bras. He'd called it a "woman's thing." She felt special. Then she spotted him sitting on a bench surrounded by pots of spring flowers—daffodils. His expression reminded her of Kevin Bernard's face the time his mind went blank during a violin recital. Confused. Lost. Embarrassed. S.B. had never seen her father look that way. It made her uncomfortable.

"I think I'll give Brenda a call one of these days soon," he'd said on the ride home from the mall. "I haven't talked to her in a while."

Although he didn't suggest the violin camp until a month later, S.B. wondered now if his idea to send her to Brenda's might have come to him that day. It all started with those bras. They'd made her feel grown-up. She *was* growing up. Was that why her father was upset?

"Do you think Brenda would like some zucchini for dinner?" Cally called through the screen. "I've got some nice ones in my garden."

S.B. came back out on the porch. "You know Brenda. She likes every food that's ever been invented."

Cally carefully placed the postcard in her shorts pocket. "I've got ones as long as my arm that would be great for stuffing. And there are some tiny ones that are so tender you can eat them raw," she said. "I'll let you pick out the best one, S.B."

They headed up the dirt road. S.B. hoped that Cally's parents wouldn't be home. After what had happened the night of the fireworks, she preferred not to meet them. Fortunately, as they turned the bend and approached Cally's trailer, S.B. saw no one around.

"My garden is this way," said Cally, circling into the field behind the trailer. "Don't trip over anything. My father collects junk."

S.B. maneuvered around car parts, pieces of motorcycles, and broken machinery and followed the girl through the yard.

"Wait until you see my tomatoes, S.B.," called Cally, as she disappeared behind the trailer. "They're as big as—Oh no!"

"What is it?" said S.B., running toward her.

Cally stood at the edge of her garden. Her shoulders were slumped. Her head was bowed.

S.B. looked at the garden. It was a square, about ten feet on each side. Except for a couple of footpaths, the entire area was covered with green plants—or had been until something had broken off all the tall plants and pulled out most of the smaller ones. Tomatoes lay on the ground, smashed. Zucchinis were cracked open. Beans had been stripped from the plants. S.B. couldn't see a single intact vegetable.

"It . . . it must have been the deer," said Cally. The girl seemed as crushed and wilted as the lettuce.

S.B. saw tears on her cheeks. "Maybe we can fix it," she said.

Cally shook her head. "It's too late for that. Everything's withered and dead already."

S.B. didn't know what to say. Cally had been working on her garden all summer, and now it was ruined. "I'll help you clean it up," she offered.

"No," Cally said softly.

Then, as S.B. bent down to pick up a stem of a broken bean plant, she noticed marks in the soft soil. They were small tire marks, like those of a motorcycle. S.B. glanced at Cally and realized that she had seen the tire marks, too. No deer had destroyed the vegetable garden, and Cally knew it.

Brenda had just finished making the hamburger patties when S.B. opened the back screen door. "You're white as a marshmallow," said the Kiwi. "You must be starved."

"It's not that," said S.B. as she washed her hands at the kitchen sink. "Cally's garden got trashed."

"Trashed? How?" asked Brenda.

"She said it was deer," replied S.B. "But I saw tire marks in the dirt. I think it was a motorcycle."

"Oh my." Brenda put her hand to her mouth. "That garden means a lot to Cally."

"Do you think her father might have done it?" asked S.B.

"What did Cally think?"

"She didn't say much," replied S.B. "She was kind of in a daze."

Brenda put her arm around S.B.'s shoulders. "Poor Cally. Her life isn't easy."

"But why would he ruin her garden?" asked S.B. "You should have seen it, Brenda. It couldn't have been an accident."

"I can't explain it," said the Kiwi, shaking her head. As Brenda gave S.B. a hug, the doorbell rang. "Who could that be at this hour?" she said. She peeked around the wall, toward the front of the house.

"Who is it?" asked S.B.

"Bad news, that's who," replied Brenda.

S.B. heard Finis thunder down the stairs and fling open the screen door. A moment later he appeared in the kitchen, followed by the tall and angular Dr. Armstrong, who was dressed in a black suit and tie. Even in the bright light of Brenda's kitchen, his eyes looked dark and shadowy.

"Dr. Armstrong has a petition for you to sign," said Finis.

"Mind if I sit down?" said the man, nodding to Brenda and S.B.

"What kind of petition?" Brenda planted herself between the table and the doorway, so that Armstrong couldn't get near a chair.

"The property value of every home in the neighborhood is threatened by Ogden Peleg's fence—and I use the word 'fence' loosely." Armstrong took a paper from the leather case he was carrying. "I'm sure that you'll join your neighbors on Skunk Hollow Road and sign this petition, which demands the enforcement of zoning laws in this township." He clicked his pen and held it out to Brenda.

"Which zoning laws?" asked Brenda.

"He erected a structure too close to the property line," said Armstrong. "That's illegal."

"From what I hear, you may have broken a few laws yourself," said Brenda.

"What do you mean?"

"Well, Harry, I went to see Old Ogden yesterday," said Brenda, putting her hands on her hips. "And he claims that those trees that you cut down a couple weeks ago were on *his* property."

"That's ludicrous," said Dr. Armstrong. "Surely you don't believe that. Face it, Brenda. The man is old and his mind isn't what it should be."

"There's nothing wrong with Old Ogden's mind." She stepped toward him. "I wouldn't sign your petition if you paid me, which you'd probably do if you thought it would work."

"Brenda!" cried Finis.

"It's all right, Finis," said Armstrong, putting

his hand on the boy's shoulder. "It doesn't matter. I already have four signatures. I'm sure the others will sign as well." He stuffed his petition into his briefcase and strode from the kitchen.

Finis swung around and glared at Brenda. "I can't believe you're standing up for Old Ogden," he said. He hurried after Dr. Armstrong, slamming the front screen door behind him.

"Why did you let Finis go?" asked S.B.

"He has to find out about Armstrong on his own," replied Brenda. "The more I say against the man, the longer it'll take Finis to see the truth." She shook her head. "I could never trust a man who kept brains in jars and dressed like an undertaker."

"I don't understand why everyone is getting so upset over some stupid trees," said S.B.

"Those trees meant a lot to Old Ogden," said Brenda. "The same way Cally's garden is special to her."

S.B. remembered the way Old Ogden had ranted and raved about the tree stumps near his bird box. The look in his eyes that day hadn't been much different from the look in Cally's when she saw her destroyed garden. Maybe Brenda was right.

"If they really were his trees," said S.B., "then Old Ogden could sue Dr. Armstrong."

"That won't get his trees back," said Brenda. "Some of those old oaks were probably there when Old Ogden's parents bought that land." She put the plates on the table. "If you want my opinion, I think Old Ogden aims to get even. That's why he put up that horrible fence. He knew it would irritate the daylights out of Harry Armstrong. And he was right."

"What will happen if everybody signs the petition?" asked S.B.

"Hard to say," said Brenda. She opened the oven door and slipped in the burgers. "I'll tell you one thing, though. I'm not going to let Harry Armstrong get away with anything. If those trees really were Old Ogden's, then Armstrong has some explaining to do."

S.B. watched her cousin slice the cucumbers for their salad. Brenda was tough. S.B. liked the way she had stood there, solid as a boulder, confronting Armstrong. She hadn't been a delicate, easily bruised kiwi fruit. Brenda was hard. She didn't break. And when she flung herself at someone, he felt it. No more Kiwi, S.B. decided. Brenda was a coconut: sweet on the inside, but with a shell as hard as rock.

Enchanter's Evil

URING THE NEXT week S.B. found out that when the Coconut got mad, she could put up quite a fight. The woman spent hours talking on the phone and gathering information to help Old Ogden. Unfortunately, Brenda's activities upset the routine of the household, which didn't please S.B. Dinner was always late. Boos and Balloons orders piled up. And Finis, who claimed that Armstrong had every right to protest the fence, spent most of his time out of the house. When he was home, he avoided Brenda like the plague.

"Why are you doing all this, Brenda?" asked S.B. on Cleaning Day while they were scrubbing the kitchen floor. "It's only a fence. It's not worth all the time you're putting into it."

"Old Ogden doesn't understand the legal issues," said Brenda. "Someone has to make sure that he isn't taken advantage of. I don't think the poor man realizes how much trouble Armstrong could make for him."

"Like what?" S.B. dumped a bucket of dirty water down the sink.

"Not only does he want the fence torn down," said Brenda, "but he wants the town to fine Old Ogden. Can you imagine the injustice of that? Armstrong cuts down Old Ogden's trees, and Old Ogden has to pay a fine." She tossed her scrub brush into the bucket and awkwardly pushed herself to her feet. "I just wish Harry Armstrong would keep Finis out of this." S.B. noticed that Brenda's smiling creases were gone.

The back door creaked open, and Cally stuck in her head. "Can I walk on the floor?"

"We haven't waxed yet," said Brenda. "Come on in."

Taking off her baseball cap, Cally crossed the floor and gave Brenda a hug.

"I haven't seen you for a while," Brenda said, giving the girl a squeeze. "How have you been, kiddo?"

"Okay," she said softly. "Except I won't be able to bring you any more zucchini this summer. You'll have to settle for the supermarket pulp."

"I heard about your garden." Brenda gently patted her back. "You'll plant another one next year."

Cally shook her head. "I don't think so."

Brenda wrapped her arms around Cally again. The girl buried her face against the Coconut's body. She didn't move for several minutes.

"Why'd he have to do that?" said Cally, her voice muffled by Brenda's blouse.

"Don't let it break you down, kiddo," said the Coconut, in her peachy voice. "Keep looking ahead. You're going to grow lots more zucchini, no matter what happens up there."

"How?" sobbed Cally. "He keeps wrecking everything."

"You're strong, kiddo." Brenda smoothed her white hair. "Nobody's going to wreck what's inside you. You're going to be fine."

As S.B. stared at Cally's quivering thin shoulders, she thought how frail the girl looked. But S.B. knew that Brenda was right. Cally was strong on the inside.

"Maybe Cally could stay for dinner," S.B. suggested.

"A wonderful idea!" said Brenda. She lifted Cally's chin. "What do you say we have a little party? I'll make a pizza, and then we can play a game of Trivial Pursuit. Finis would like that."

Brenda was clever, thought S.B. Not only would she cheer up Cally, but she'd also get Finis to hang around by tempting him with pizza and his favorite game.

"How about it, Cally?" asked S.B.

Smiling, she nodded. "I like eating here."

"Good girl," said Brenda. "We'll get some meat on those bones of yours tonight." She opened the refrigerator. "Now, I'd say it's about time we took a lemonade break."

"I'm dying of thirst," said S.B. quickly, before Brenda could spot another dirty area on the floor for her to scrub.

After they each had a glassful, Brenda handed S.B. an empty cup and said, "How about taking some lemonade out to Finis? I bet he's ready for a drink."

Cally picked up the pitcher of lemonade, and the two girls went out to the front lawn where Finis was mowing.

"Since when does anybody bring me lemonade?" said Finis, as he turned off the lawn mower.

"It was Brenda's idea," said S.B., handing him the plastic cup. "Take a hint, Finis."

"What hint?" He emptied the cup in one gulp and held it out for a refill. Cally poured him more.

"Brenda's trying to make peace with you over this stupid tree fight," said S.B. "She wants you to stay out of the whole thing."

"Why do I have to stay out of it when she's in it up to her eyebrows?"

"She thinks that Old Ogden needs a friend," said S.B. "What's wrong with that?"

"Maybe Dr. Armstrong needs a friend, too," said Finis.

"But he's . . . he's creepy, Finis," said S.B.

"What do you know, anyway?" he snapped. Handing her his cup, he stomped back to the mower.

"You're wrong to be *his* friend," said Cally. "We're only trying to protect you from being corrupted by the Enchanter's magic."

S.B. was surprised to hear Cally drift into her story.

Finis glanced at S.B., then back to Cally. "What are you talking about?"

"You don't understand, Water," said Cally. "The Enchanter has unleashed a black cloud of evil. It is growing and spreading throughout the kingdom."

"The only thing I see growing is this grass," said Finis, as he bent over the mower.

"The first to be poisoned are the weak. They become possessed with a wickedness never before seen in the kingdom." Cally clenched her fists. Her chin trembled. "It makes them act in cruel and unspeakable ways. I know. I have seen it. Beware, or you too will be a victim of the Enchanter's evil." Wiping her hand across her eyes, she turned and ran into the house.

"What's wrong with her?" asked Finis. "What's this about the weak being poisoned?"

"I think she means her father," said S.B. "He rode through her garden with his motorcycle and killed all her vegetables."

"And you think you've got problems with *your* father," he said.

"*My* father would never deliberately do something that mean to me," said S.B. indignantly.

"I don't know about that." Finis pulled the starter on the mower. "The way you tell it, he's a real jerk."

"The part about him making me come here this summer . . . Well, I'm not so mad about that anymore," she said. "I think he might have had his reasons."

"That's a news flash," shouted Finis over the roar of the engine.

It was news to S.B., too. She hadn't realized until that moment that she'd forgotten to feel angry with her father for nearly a week.

The Coconut's plot to lure Finis out of his room worked. When she pulled out the Trivial Pursuit board that evening, he was hooked. S.B. didn't expect to do well at the game, but she enjoyed playing. Cally, who read all the time, knew about half of her questions. The real experts were Brenda and Finis.

"You're winning because you're older," Finis said to Brenda after she had won her fourth wedge. "It gives you an advantage because you lived through all the things they ask about."

"Let's not be nasty," said Brenda, smiling. "Can't you give me credit for my superb memory?"

"Yeah," said Finis. "I guess the Civil War must seem like yesterday to you."

"He doesn't like to lose, does he, girls?" Brenda nudged S.B. with her elbow. "Roll the dice, Finis. It's your turn."

The phone rang and Finis sprang to answer it.

"Saved by the bell." Cally laughed.

"It only delays his humiliation," said Brenda. "I aim to win this game."

Finis came back to the kitchen. "For you, Brenda."

Brenda motioned for them to play on without her. When S.B.'s turn came, she missed her question—again.

"The S.B. must not be for Super Brain," said Finis, pointing to her empty playing piece.

"Don't let him tease you," said Cally. "He plays this game so much, he knows most of the questions by heart."

"Or maybe it's Slightly Baffled," he continued.

"Maybe you're First In Nonsense, Ignorance, and Stupidity," said S.B.

Finis clicked his tongue. "Not bad, S.B. I'll have to remember that one."

Brenda returned and sat down at the table. "That was Mildred, a friend of mine who works over in the town zoning office," she said. "She told me that Dr. Armstrong and Old Ogden were notified in today's mail that the maps and deeds showing the boundary line between their properties are unclear. The zoning board is requesting a new survey before they make a decision."

"What does that mean?" asked Finis. "They're going to make Old Ogden take down the fence, aren't they?"

"It means that they won't make Old Ogden do anything until they're sure where the property line is," replied Brenda. "If it turns out that the fence is in far enough on Old Ogden's land, the way he says it is, then Dr. Armstrong doesn't— as they say—have a leg to stand on."

"You don't have to look so happy about it." Finis pushed his chair back and stood up. "I think it stinks."

"Let's forget about all that and finish our game," said Brenda.

"I don't feel like playing anymore." He turned and went upstairs.

Brenda sighed. "Here we go again."

"Don't worry," said S.B. "Remember what you told me before? 'He'll be out of his funk by morning.'"

Brenda chuckled. "I did say that, didn't I?" She put her playing piece back in the box. "Do you two mind if I stop? I'd like to give Old Ogden a call before he goes to bed."

After they put the game away, Cally pulled S.B. outside into the carport. "Brenda's phone call was a bad omen," she said in a low voice.

"Why did you want to come out here?" said

S.B. "The bugs are horrible." She smacked at a mosquito on her arm.

"I don't want Finis to hear." Cally looked up at his bedroom window above the carport. "If he knows what we're planning, he'll never cooperate. Without him, everything will go wrong."

"What *are* we planning?" said S.B.

Cally reached into the pocket of her purple shorts and pulled out the pink stone. Even in the dim light of the carport, the tiny flecks of white in the rock sparkled. "The amulet helps me to see more clearly what will be," she said. "Listen and remember." She grasped S.B.'s hand and closed her eyes.

"I'm listening," whispered S.B. Despite her reluctance to play the Story when Brenda or Finis might come out of the house at any moment, S.B. closed her eyes and let Cally's voice pull her into the other world.

"From the beginning, the Enchanter has planned to conquer the kingdom," began Earth. "He wants to change it. He wants to leave his evil mark upon it. He will not allow anything to interfere with his plans. But the Lord of the Green Realm did not see this when he allowed the Enchanter to enter the kingdom. It was a serious error."

"The Green Lord let him in?" asked Air.

"Yes," replied Earth. "The Green Lord was the only one who had the power to open the kingdom to the Enchanter. He was deceived by the Enchanter. He believed the lies and promises."

"What about the Lady of the Pines?" asked Air. "Why didn't she prevent the Enchanter from coming?"

"The Lady has wisdom, but she does not have the power to stop the Enchanter's evil alone. That is why we must help her."

"We?"

"You and I, Air. And Water. Especially Water." The light shining on Earth's white hair created a glowing halo around her head. "The Enchanter is angry because the Green Lord's magic is stronger than he expected. The Green Lord's mystical barrier, full of magic from his castle, has threatened the Enchanter's power," she continued. "The time of greatest danger for the Green Lord—and for the kingdom—has come."

"But the Green Lord has great magic. Can't he protect himself without our help?" asked Air. She secretly feared the power of the Green Lord, but she did not want Earth to know.

"The Green Lord is blind to the danger. He does not see the intense malevolence within the Enchanter." Earth hesitated. "But I, Earth, have seen the dark evil. I, Earth, know the destruction

and ruin it brings. We must not let the Enchanter's evil spread any further." Earth was silent
for a moment. "The Enchanter will work his spell
at night, when he can conceal himself and when
the Green Lord is off his guard. We must keep
watch over the Green Lord. We must protect him
from the Enchanter's magic, or great harm will
come to him. It is up to us, Air."

Cally opened her eyes and released S.B.'s hand.
The two girls stared at each other. S.B. took a
deep breath and blinked. She felt prickly, as if every nerve in her skin had been activated.

Cally put the amulet back in her pocket.
"Meet me at the Twisted Tree at midnight," she
whispered. "And make sure Finis is there."

"How in blazes am I going to do that?" S.B.
called to her as she walked away. But Cally had
already disappeared into the shadows.

14

Light and Flame

S.B. LAY IN her bed, staring through the window at the moon and wondering what she should do. It was eleven-thirty. Cally expected her at the Twisted Tree in a half hour. S.B. couldn't decide whether she should meet her.

Her mind was full of questions. How much of Cally's story was real and how much was her imagination? Was her warning merely another part of her fairy tale? Or was Old Ogden in real danger from Dr. Armstrong, just as the Green Lord was from the Enchanter? Did it really matter whether she joined Cally that night?

She knew what Finis would say if she

marched into his room and announced that they had to save the Green Lord. He had lost interest in the Story ever since Cally mentioned the Enchanter to him. He'd never agree to tromp around in the woods in the middle of the night playing the Story.

S.B. wasn't keen about wandering around in the woods, either. The full moon, glowing in the night sky, cast eerie shadows on the walls of her room. The forest shadows would be even spookier.

Despite her own doubts, S.B. was sure that Cally was absolutely serious about her story. She'd be waiting at the Twisted Tree and counting on S.B. to show up—with Finis. Even if the whole thing turned out to be pretend, S.B. didn't want to let Cally down.

She tossed off her sheets, changed into a T-shirt and shorts, and quietly slipped into the hall. Finis and Brenda had gone to bed almost two hours earlier and the house was still. Being careful not to wake the Coconut, S.B. turned the knob of Finis's door. She knew it wouldn't be locked. Brenda didn't allow locked doors at night, in case there was a fire.

Slipping into his room, S.B. closed the door behind her. The moonlight streamed through the window and left a pool of brightness in the middle of the floor. Finis lay half-covered on the bed, with his shirt off. S.B. reached down and gently touched his arm.

He awoke with a start. "What are you doing in here?" Sitting up, he pulled the sheet to his chin.

"Shush." S.B. put a finger to her lips.

"Get out!" he growled.

S.B. crouched beside his bed. "It's a full moon," she whispered. "I want you to take me owling."

"Are you nuts?"

"You said you would," she said. "Remember?"

"I was only kidding around with you. Take off." He lay down and faced the wall.

"I bet you've never been owling in your life," said S.B. "You're probably afraid to go out in the dark." She knew which of them was afraid, but she tried not to think about it.

"I've been owling lots of times," said Finis. "I just don't feel like it tonight. I'm tired."

"I think you're afraid that Brenda will catch you," said S.B.

Finis sat up again. "I've snuck out plenty," he said. "She's never caught me yet."

"Then let's go," said S.B. "It's a perfect night for owling."

"Since when are you an expert?"

"Well, isn't it?" S.B. stepped away from his bed until she stood in the patch of moonlight.

Finis made an annoyed grunt. "If you want me to get dressed, wait in the hall."

They left the house without Brenda waking up. Finis, it turned out, had perfected the art of sneaking out at night. He led S.B. through his window onto the carport roof. With little difficulty, they climbed down the wall of firewood, using the spaces between the logs as toe grips.

Once they were outside, the excitement of the adventure seemed to capture Finis. Warning S.B. to avoid the gravel driveway, where their footsteps would be noisy, he hurried across the lawn. When she passed the glass ball, S.B. noticed that it glowed as the moonlight struck the mirrored surface. She glanced back at the dark house, then ran to catch up with Finis.

They had walked a short way up the dirt road when Finis turned to enter the woods.

"Wait," called S.B. "We can't go in there."

He glanced back over his shoulder at her. "Why not?"

"We . . . we have to stay on the road."

"Owls don't hang out on roads, stupid," said Finis.

She couldn't tell him that they had to meet Cally at the Twisted Tree. "I've never been that way," she said. "Since it's dark, I'd feel more comfortable on the other path you showed me."

"You're real adventurous, aren't you, S.B.?" he muttered. "Okay, we'll go the other way."

As they walked up the hill, lightning bugs flashed around them. The air hummed with the murmur of insects. Occasionally, S.B. heard crackles from the woods on either side of the road. She thought of the lurking creatures hiding in the moon shadows.

Finis stopped at the Twisted Tree. "We'll go in here. It's a pretty good place for owls."

S.B. peered up the road into the shadows. There was no sign of Cally. She glanced at her watch. It was a few minutes before midnight. She strained to hear the sound of Cally's footsteps coming down the hill.

"Come on," said Finis. "We don't have all night."

She couldn't ask him to wait for Cally. If he knew she was coming, he'd realize that the night walk had something to do with the Story. He'd head home immediately.

"Well, I'm going," said Finis. "You can come if you want."

S.B. suddenly thought that maybe Cally had no intention of meeting them there that night. She knew that S.B. didn't like the woods. Maybe it was all a big joke—on S.B.

No, S.B. decided. Cally wasn't the kind of person to pull a mean trick like that. Besides, earlier in the evening she had talked as if she truly believed the Green Lord was in danger. Cally wanted to help him. She must have been delayed. She would come.

As a sign to her, S.B. dropped a wadded-up tissue from her shorts pocket on the dirt road by the Twisted Tree. Then she jumped the ditch behind Finis.

She stared into the dark woods. Most of the moonlight was blocked by the leaves. The branches of the trees seemed to reach for her like grotesque arms. Her feet refused to move.

"Aren't you coming?" Finis called to her. "Or does S.B. stand for Scared Baby?"

She couldn't back out now. She had to follow him, despite her fear. As she watched him enter the woods, S.B. thought of a way to find courage. She would pretend that she was the brave, brilliant, and adventurous Air on a mission to save the Green Lord. But could she travel into the Story without Cally to lead her?

She closed her eyes and let her mind drift...

Air plunged into the woods behind Water. With him in the lead, the two adventurers moved farther into the Wild Wood. The beasts of the kingdom let them pass, for they knew that the two were on an important mission—a mission to save the Lord of the Green Realm from the Enchanter.

Every hundred feet, Water stopped and motioned for Air to be quiet. *"Whoo-whoo-who-who,"* he called.

Air knew that Water, who had the power to speak with the beasts of the Wood, was asking for information about the Green Lord. There was no reply from the Great Bird. They went on.

They approached the path to the Tangled Jungle. "This way," Air said to her companion.

He turned to look where she pointed. "Why there?" he asked.

He was the Way-finder. If Air offended him, he might refuse to follow her. And he *must* go with her to the Green Lord's lands if their mission was to succeed. "I heard an owl over there," she said.

"Impossible," he replied. "I didn't hear it."

"I did. We should go that way."

Water hesitated but finally changed course. They headed for the Tangled Jungle.

It was dark as pitch there. Not a single beam of moonlight penetrated the thick roof of vines. Twigs snapped. Leaves swished. Air wondered if they were being followed by beasts loyal to the Enchanter. Then she remembered that the Tangled Jungle was protected by the Magic. They would be safe.

Water knew the way even in darkness. Air stayed close behind him, holding the hem of his cloak, until a gleam of moonlight appeared at the other end of the Tangled Jungle. The Gorge of Death, black and deep, stretched before them.

"Where now?" asked Water. He was impatient.

"We must cross the Gorge," came a voice from behind them in the Tangled Jungle.

Water and Air, both alarmed by the voice, screamed.

Earth emerged from the shadows of the Tangled Jungle. "Do not be afraid," she said. "It is I, your friend Earth. You have done well, Air, to bring Water."

"I should have known what you two were up to," said Water, as he pushed past Earth. "I'm going back."

"No, don't," pleaded Earth. "Look. Do you not see the Dryads beckoning to us? The Green Lord needs our protection."

Air looked across the Gorge of Death, past the shadows of the trees, toward the Green Lord's lands. She could see the Mystical Barrier and the remains of the Magical Castle. And suddenly she saw. The flash of red. The curl of white smoke. The tall, dark figure running from the Mystical Barrier and disappearing into the shadows. She could feel her heartbeat in her ears. She reached for Water's arm.

The clearing was bathed in the red glow of the fire. The flames danced into the night sky, fueled by the ancient dry wood of Old Ogden's fence. "Finis!" shouted S.B., pulling on his arm.

Finis stared across the gorge.

"It's the Enchanter's evil," said Cally. "We have to stop it before the kingdom is destroyed." She jumped across the gorge.

The fire moved quickly down the length of the fence, spitting red sparks as it spread. "Come on, Finis," said S.B., brushing her hair from her face. "There's a wind picking up. Do you feel it? We have to warn Old Ogden and call the fire department."

"Looks like the old guy already knows," replied Finis, pointing across the gorge.

Old Ogden was hurrying from his house toward the burning fence. Cally ran after him.

Finis stepped to the edge of the gorge and leaped across. On the other side, he stood on the edge so that S.B. could see where to aim her jump. Taking a deep breath and a running start, she sprang across. When she landed, she lost her balance and fell to her knees on the edge. Finis reached down and pulled her up.

As they ran across the clearing together, the heat of the fire smacked S.B. in the face. The entire fence was burning. When they reached Cally, she was less than ten feet from the fire. She stood over Old Ogden, tugging at his arm.

"What happened?" asked S.B.

"He tripped over something," answered Cally. "I warned him not to go any closer."

"Did you call the fire department?" shouted Finis over the roar of the fire.

Old Ogden nodded. "Get me up!" he yelled.

Finis put his arm around the old man's waist as Old Ogden tried to stand. But his leg wouldn't hold him.

"It might be broken," said S.B. "We'd better be careful with him."

"Let's get him under the arms," said Finis. He leaned close to Old Ogden's ear. "Keep your weight off your leg. We're going to pull you away from the fire."

But Old Ogden pushed Finis's hands off. "No! I have to get the eggs!"

"He's talking crazy." Finis grabbed him under the arms again. "Shut up, old man, and let us help you."

"I think he's talking about the bluebird eggs," shouted S.B. She felt the fire's heat on her back.

"Where are they, Air?" asked Cally. "We must rescue them for the Green Lord."

"Over there." S.B. pointed to the bird box nailed to a tree a few feet from the burning fence.

Old Ogden struggled to raise himself off the ground again, but fell back. "Stay off that leg," said Finis.

"Got to save the eggs!" Old Ogden cried.

"He won't go unless we get the nest," said S.B.

"I'll get them," Cally said to the old man. "But you'll have to let us move you."

"Wait, Cally," called S.B. "You're too short to reach the box. I'll do it." Wishing at that moment that she were truly as brave as Air, S.B. covered her face with her arms, ducked her head against the heat, and ran toward the bird box. As quickly as she could, she yanked open the door of the box and gently lifted out the nest. The mother bird had flown away, but the five blue eggs lay safely in the nest.

By that time Finis and Cally had managed to drag Old Ogden across the grass to the middle of the clearing, away from the fire. Wiping the sweat from her forehead, S.B. sprinted back toward them. When she glanced behind her and saw how close she'd been to the flames, her stomach flip-flopped.

"You could have gotten us all killed trying to save a bunch of stupid eggs," Finis said to Old Ogden.

"He was only trying to protect the creatures of his kingdom," said Cally, taking the nest from S.B. and setting it in her hat. She handed the hat to Old Ogden.

He pulled a large white handkerchief from his overalls pocket and laid it over the nest. Looking up at S.B., he said, "Thank you, girl."

A siren cut through the roar and crackle of the fire. S.B. spotted a rotating blue light on the road beyond the burning fence. In a few moments a dozen firefighters swarmed into the clearing. One hurried toward them.

"We're going to need more water than the truck carries," the man shouted. "With this wind, if we don't wet down the trees and brush, the fire will spread. Is there a pond around?"

"There's a stream over there," Finis said, pointing behind Old Ogden's house. "I can show you."

"It's worth a try," said the firefighter.

After Finis and the man had run off, a second firefighter approached. "What happened to him?" the woman asked, kneeling over Old Ogden.

S.B. caught her breath. The old man's eyes were closed and his arm lay limp across his chest. "Is . . . is he dead?" she asked.

"Unconscious." The firefighter laid a blanket over him.

"He fell and hurt his leg," said Cally, picking up the nest-filled hat from his lap.

"The ankle feels broken," said the woman, as she ran her hands over the bone. "He must have passed out." She talked on her radio, and in a few minutes another firefighter arrived with a stretcher. They carried Old Ogden toward the road.

Within a half hour the volunteer fire department had drowned the fire on the fence and wet down the surrounding trees. The three—S.B., Finis, and Cally—stood in the clearing, next to the skeleton of Old Ogden's barn. It was dark and quiet now that the fire trucks had gone. But they could still smell the choking odor of smoke.

"That's the end of the fence," said S.B., staring at the burned area. Dr. Armstrong's house, visible between the trees, was dark. It looked as if no one was home. S.B. knew the darkness was a deception. He was in there. She had seen him run toward the house.

"The bluebird box was destroyed," said Cally. She looked at the nest in her hands. "You saved the eggs from the Enchanter's fire, Air."

"The Story's over, Cally," said Finis. "Stop playing it."

"It's never over, Finis. Not really," she replied. "You saw that Dr. Armstrong was the Enchanter, didn't you? He wanted to get rid of the fence, so he set it on fire."

Finis looked toward Armstrong's house. "I don't understand why he did that," he said. "He almost burned the woods down, too."

"You don't understand," said Cally, "because you saw only his good side. He let you help him in his lab and he gave you work. But he hid his other side from you."

Finis stared at Armstrong's house for a long time without speaking. Then he turned away and headed across the clearing. "We'd better get back before Brenda misses us," he said to S.B. "She's going to have a fit if she finds out we were over here."

S.B. started to follow, but Cally took her arm. "He saw," she said. "Now he knows."

"Is that why you wanted him here tonight?" asked S.B.

"Yes," replied Cally, as she cradled the bird nest in her arms. "The Enchanter was angry. I had a feeling he would perform an evil act. I wanted Water to witness it, so he would believe."

"But how did you know it would be tonight?" asked S.B.

Cally looked into the sky. "Because of the power of the full moon." She smiled at S.B. "You were brave and true tonight, Air. I knew I could depend on you."

As she walked back to Brenda's, S.B. thought about the Story. Was it real, or was it just fantasy? S.B. wasn't sure. But after what had happened that night, the answer no longer seemed important.

15

Departure

T HE KIDS WRAPPED the eggs in an electric blanket last night," said Brenda. She nodded at S.B., Finis, and Cally, who stood a few feet away from Old Ogden's porch.

"Well, I'm glad they had the sense," grumbled the old man. He sat in a chair with his leg propped on a stool.

"Too bad *you* didn't have more sense," said Brenda. "Then you wouldn't have that broken ankle."

"Wouldn't have happened if he hadn't been up to no good!" Old Ogden pointed across the clearing to Armstrong's house. "You kids saw him, didn't you? You know what I'm talking about. He aimed to burn us all out."

"You promised me you'd calm down about that and let the sheriff handle it," said Brenda.

"What do you want us to do with the eggs, Mr. Peleg?" asked Cally, as she laid the nest, still cradled in her baseball hat, in his lap.

"They need to be in a new box right away." He gently placed his hand over the eggs. "Otherwise, the parents will leave for good."

"These children can build one," said Brenda.

Old Ogden grunted.

"You might find out that they're not such bad company." Brenda smiled.

"We'll see," snapped Old Ogden. He pointed to a shed behind his house. "Wood, saw, and hammer are in there."

"I've got to say this for him," Finis said to S.B. and Cally as they walked around the end of the porch, "he's tough for an old guy."

"My hearing's good, too," called Old Ogden. "And I'll tell you something, boy. It's going to take more than a little fall to keep me down."

With Old Ogden barking instructions, the three of them managed to construct the bird box. S.B. measured, Finis sawed, and Cally hammered.

"Not bad," said Old Ogden, as he examined the finished product. "Now let's get it up."

"Where should it go?" asked S.B., looking at the charred remains of the fence and nearby brush.

"Well, thanks to our neighbor," said Old Ogden, "there isn't much left to hang it on."

"Stop your growling," said Brenda, as she adjusted the pillow under his foot. "I told you we'll get that survey done and prove the land is yours. Then Armstrong will have to pay to have those bushes and trees replanted."

"That's not going to do these eggs much good now, is it?" said Old Ogden.

"How about putting the box on the trunk of that tree by the gorge?" suggested Finis. "There's plenty of cover for the birds there, but it's far enough away from branches that no predators will be able to climb into it."

Old Ogden leaned forward in his chair. "It's about all there is, I guess."

S.B. and Finis found wire in the shed. By wrapping the wire around the tree trunk, they managed to attach the bird box to the tree. Cally set the nest and its five blue eggs in the box and shut the tiny wooden door.

"I can't say I'm overjoyed that you three were roaming around in the woods last night," said Brenda, when they returned to the porch. "But I'm glad you helped out our friend Mr. Peleg."

"It was because of Cally," said S.B. "She was watching out for him."

"Is that right?" Old Ogden looked at Cally. "Well, I guess I should thank you for saving the eggs."

Cally walked over to his chair. "I was noticing that clearing of yours, Mr. Peleg," she said, resting her hand on his shoulder. "You know, it would be a perfect spot for a vegetable garden. It isn't too late in the season to put in fall peas and spinach. You like them, don't you?"

"What a lovely idea, Cally," said Brenda. "That's just what you need, Mr. Peleg. A nice garden. Fact is, I remember that you used to have one years ago."

Old Ogden pulled at his white beard. "It got to be too much work."

"But I'll do the work," said Cally. "Finis could help, too. Wouldn't you, Finis?"

"Maybe," he said, glancing toward Armstrong's house. "I guess I'll have some extra time on my hands now."

"You get tired of that grocery-store produce, don't you?" said Brenda. "I bet you miss your garden, Mr. Peleg."

"Now, don't you go telling me what I miss and what I don't miss," he replied.

"Look," said S.B., pointing at a streak of blue near the bird box.

Old Ogden squinted. "Oho! It's the male bluebird. The female must be close."

"Does that mean they'll stay and hatch the eggs?" asked S.B.

"It's a good sign," said Old Ogden. He smiled and sat back in his chair. "A real good sign."

"About the garden, Mr. Peleg," said Brenda. "After all, the children have been very helpful to you today, wouldn't you say?"

Old Ogden pointed a finger at Cally and Finis. "I don't want any shenanigans around my place," he said. "You'll do it my way, understand?"

Cally smiled. "Okay, Mr. Peleg."

Brenda put her arm around the girl's shoulders. "It's settled, then," she said. "Why not break ground today?"

Over the next several days, S.B. helped Cally and Finis dig up the ground in the clearing for the garden. By the end of the week, the bluebird eggs had hatched, and Cally began to plant her seeds. Even Old Ogden seemed pleased as he watched from his porch.

"I'm glad you're getting a new garden to take care of," said S.B., as she and Cally walked back to Brenda's after putting in the peas. "It wasn't fair that you lost your other garden."

Cally kicked a stone on the shoulder of the dirt road. "I'm not going to sit back and let bad things ruin my life. Even if my thread of life is gray and coarse, I'm going to turn it into gold." She turned to S.B. "Brenda helped me see that I could do that."

"She helped me see some things, too," said S.B.

As they crossed Brenda's lawn, S.B. stopped at the mirrored ball—the Magic Sphere. Walking slowly around it, she watched the colors of the reflected flowers and trees blend together in strange, distorted collages.

"Things can look different. It depends on where you stand," said Cally, coming up behind her. "Just like the story about your mother. Brenda helped you see it in another way, didn't she?"

S.B. nodded. "I always thought my mother didn't want me. But Brenda says that she tried to take me with her. My dad stopped her because he didn't think it would be good for me to travel around the country."

"If you hadn't come this summer," said Cally, "you might never have known about that."

"I think my dad wanted me to hear the other side of the story," said S.B., glancing back at the glass ball. "I just wish he hadn't been so tricky about it. He made me feel like he was ditching me."

"I'm sure he didn't mean to," said Cally, as they sat down on the porch step.

"I guess he wants to do everything right," said S.B., "even though a lot of the time he does it wrong."

"It all turned out right, though, S.B.," said Cally. "That's what matters." She looked toward the sun. "If the weather is decent, we should be eating lettuce and spinach by mid-September. I wish you'd be here to share them."

"I never thought I'd say this, but I do too," replied S.B. The month that she had feared would drag on forever was over, instead, in a blink.

Postcards from her father—five of them—came the next day. Brenda brought them in from the mailbox as S.B. and Finis were eating lunch.

"I think Lucille down at the post office spends so much time reading our mail that she forgets to deliver it," said the Coconut, handing the cards to S.B. "Good thing they came today, or you would have missed getting them."

S.B. stuck the cards in her rear pocket.

"I've got some other good news, too," said Brenda, as she made herself a sandwich. "I talked to my attorney friend, Walt, the one who agreed to help out Old Ogden. He had a survey done this week, and it turns out those trees were on Ogden's land all along."

"That means Dr. Armstrong had no right to cut them down," interrupted S.B. "Just like you said, Brenda."

"You bet your booties." Brenda winked at her. "And Walt says they have a strong case against Harry Armstrong. He's going to ask the town justice to make Armstrong plant new bushes and trees, ones as mature as can be safely transplanted."

"Big trees cost big bucks," said Finis.

"This is true," said Brenda. "But Walt thinks that Armstrong won't have much choice. He's also going to demand money for Old Ogden's medical expenses."

"But no one, except us, saw that he set the fire," said Finis.

"Armstrong knows there are witnesses," said Brenda. "My guess is that he'll be glad to cooperate as long as he doesn't get accused of arson."

"He's lucky he didn't end up in jail for what he did," said S.B.

"There's even more," Brenda went on as she sat down at the table. "When I drove by Armstrong's house this morning, I saw a realtor's car in his driveway."

"You mean he's moving?" asked S.B.

"Well, it looks like he's thinking of putting his house up for sale. I guess he's had enough of all of us."

So the Enchanter has been banished from the kingdom, thought S.B. Cally would be pleased with the news.

"It's just as well that he's leaving," muttered Finis.

"People sometimes disappoint us," said Brenda, in her peachy voice. "I'm sorry it had to happen to you this time, Finis."

"I'll live," he said, taking a bite of pickle. "By the way, S.B., did you know that a newborn baby has 144 more bones than an adult?"

"That's the first nongruesome trivia that you've told me," she replied. "I can't believe it!"

"Oops." Finis grinned. "I guess I'm slipping. Don't worry, though. I'll work on it."

Up in her room later, S.B. examined the postcards. There was one each from London, Rome, Athens, Madrid, and Copenhagen. The pictures were beautiful. The stamps were colorful. The messages were interesting, and all ended with, "I miss you. Love, Dad." S.B. remembered her vow to mutilate and burn these cards when they arrived. But her anger at her father was gone, and she didn't feel like doing it anymore.

Taking the envelope of snapshots from her violin case, she spread them on her bed. Her parents looked happy. She wished that it hadn't gone wrong between them.

She might have had brothers and sisters. Maybe her father wouldn't have worked such long hours. He might not have made a fuss about which schools she attended and how she spent her time. Her mother would have made him different. She would have made *all* of it different—if she hadn't wanted to be a star, if she hadn't left her daughter, if she hadn't been on that airplane, if she hadn't died.

S.B.'s life might have been better. Or, as Brenda would probably say, it might have been worse. S.B. would never know. That part of her life was over. There was nothing she could do to change it.

What had Cally said the night of the fireworks? *Think about what you have instead of what you've lost.* Maybe she was right. S.B. had a dad who cared about her, even though he sometimes messed up and didn't always understand how she felt. But she was better off than Cally, whose parents neither understood nor cared.

She placed the snapshots back in her violin case and hurried down the hall to Brenda's room. "Okay if I come in?" she said, knocking on the door.

"Sure," said Brenda, as she put down her book.

"You know those photographs you gave me? The ones of their wedding?" said S.B., sitting down on the bed next to her cousin. "I've decided that I'll keep them. I'll show them to my dad."

"I'm glad to hear you say that," said Brenda.

"I think I want to hear about my mother from him," said S.B. "Do you think he'd mind?"

Brenda shook her head. "I know he wouldn't mind at all."

"It's confusing to find out that someone you always thought hated you might not have," said S.B. "At least, *you* say she didn't."

"She didn't," said Brenda, as she put her arm around S.B.'s shoulders. "I know that for a fact."

"I wish she hadn't given me such a dumb name, though."

"Don't hold it against her. Your mother gave it to you for all the right reasons." Brenda gently squeezed S.B.'s arm. "She thought it was a won-derful name with a warm and happy feeling. She gave it to you because she loved you."

"I can't help that I despise it," said S.B.

"I know how you feel. What seemed special to your parents doesn't necessarily seem so good to you, right?" Brenda chuckled. "I've never been thrilled with my name, either. But I've gotten used to it. Maybe someday you will, too."

"And if I don't, I guess I can stick with the initials."

"Exactly," said Brenda. She reached into the pocket of her cotton blouse and pulled out some cash. "We need to settle up our finances before you leave."

"You mean for the Boos and Balloons poems I did?"

"Of course," said Brenda, handing her the money. "I hope you'll keep working for me after you go home. We could have one of those long-distance business relationships."

"You'd really want to do that?"

"You bet! You're a valued employee, S.B.," said Brenda. "I can't afford to lose you to the competition. But can you fit me into your busy schedule?"

"I'll make the time," said S.B., smiling.

"You know something, kiddo?" said Brenda.

"I'm sure going to miss you." She wrapped her arms around S.B. and pulled her close.

This time S.B. didn't try to wiggle away. Surrounded by Brenda's warm skin and soft cotton blouse, she felt like a caterpillar in a cozy cocoon. Her father had been right. Brenda *was* a peach. Soft and tender on the outside. And solid as a rock at the center.

"It's almost three o'clock," Brenda called from the bottom of the stairs. "We ought to be going, S.B."

The day to go home had arrived. S.B. took a final look around her room, then picked up her bags.

Cally was waiting in the kitchen. "I came to say good-bye," she said.

S.B. took the five postcards from her pocket and handed them to Cally. "I thought you might like to have these."

Cally reached into her own pocket. "And I have something to give you, S.B." She handed her a pink pebble.

"But it's your amulet," said S.B.

"I want you to keep it," said Cally. "To remember the Story."

"I thought it was special to you," said S.B., as she ran her finger over the pebble, still warm from being in the white-haired girl's pocket.

"It is," Cally replied. "But I'll find another. There are plenty here."

Carefully S.B. put the pebble in her pocket. She was glad Cally wanted her to have it. Most of all, she was glad she'd met Cally and become her friend.

"Let's get this show on the road," called Brenda. "Why don't you come to the airport with us, Cally? Finis can ride in the back of the truck."

"You mean he's coming, too?" said S.B.

"He insisted," replied Brenda, raising an eyebrow.

After S.B. said a final good-bye to Tarzan the gorilla, they all piled into Brenda's red Toyota. As they drove to the airport, S.B. thought about traveling the same route four weeks earlier.

She had never made it to the lake. The city had been a disappointment. Her violin had grown dusty. But her vacation had been exciting and interesting, just as her father promised.

She hadn't gotten used to the lurking beasts. But the trees, the quiet, the clean smells, and especially the people had grown on her. As she stood by the gate in the small airport terminal facing the three of them, S.B. felt teary.

Cally hugged her and whispered in her ear, "Farewell, Air."

"Keep going for the gold, Cally," S.B. replied.

The white-haired girl nodded and smiled.

Finis handed S.B. a small box wrapped in red paper and tied with a gold bow. "Don't open it until you're on the plane," he said.

"Thanks, Finis." Hugging *him* was out of the question. "You didn't have to give me anything."

"I wanted to," he said. "By the way, did you know that in one of the worst cases of compulsive swallowing ever recorded, a woman had over 2,500 objects in her stomach, including 947 pins?"

S.B.'s stomach suddenly felt prickly. "I see you're back in your old disgusting form again."

The Peach wrapped her fleshy arms around S.B. "Until next year, kiddo."

"You mean I can come back?"

"You bet your booties, chickadee," she said. "I'll keep a place for you at the dinner table."

After more hugs and thank-yous, S.B.'s flight was announced over the loudspeaker. Waving good-bye, she hurried down the short hall to the gate. She was almost to the X-ray machine when she heard it—loud and clear, echoing through the terminal, bouncing off the walls.

"Strawberry Field, Strawberry Field!"

Mortified, she swerved around. Finis was running toward her.

"You forgot your violin," he said, thrusting it at her.

"Why did you have to do that?" she cried. "And in front of all these people."

"It's your name, isn't it?"

"I didn't think you knew."

"I didn't until now. It was only a guess." Finis grinned. "But you just confirmed it."

S.B. clenched her teeth. "Don't ever use it again."

"Better hurry, or you'll miss your plane . . . Strawberry."

Cursing him under her breath, S.B. dropped her violin case on the conveyor belt and walked through the X-ray gate. On the other side, she turned around. "You'd better watch out, Minus Finis. I have a whole year to think of a way to get even."

"You'll need it!" he called back.

Somewhere over the Catskills, S.B. remembered Finis's present. He had been mean to catch her off guard with her name. But, she had to admit, he had been surprisingly nice to give her a going-away gift. She slipped off the ribbon and un-wrapped the box. Lifting the lid, she saw a piece of cotton. Had he given her jewelry? She gently removed the cotton.

"Awk!" she screeched, dropping the box. The man across the aisle looked over.

Burning with embarrassment, S.B. picked the box off the floor of the plane. Fortunately, it had landed upright and the contents hadn't fallen out. Finis had thought of everything. He'd wrapped it in plastic so that it would stay wet and slimy. He'd even labeled it with a piece of masking tape in case she couldn't identify his lovely gift.

She wondered if Finis's kind gesture included making the hideous creature fat and juicy on his own blood. The thought made her skin crawl.

S.B. put the lid back on, carefully rewrapped the box, and replaced the ribbon. She considered what a blood-bloated black leech would look like after a year in a box. Smiling to herself, she vowed that Finis would find out next summer.

Resting her head against the seat, she reached into her pocket and touched Cally's amulet. Then she closed her eyes.

Using the magic only she possessed, Air the Adventurer tricked the Silver Dragon into flying her far across the mountains and rivers. Her apprenticeship with the Lady of the Pines had ended. It was time to return to her homeland and her king.

With her she took Water's gift—the Black Beast. A single drop of moisture from this deadly

198 • BEYOND THE MAGIC SPHERE

creature's body was capable of killing five men. It was a weapon to be used only in moments of extreme danger. It would protect Air against the evil forces in her homeland.

But more prized than even the Black Beast was the Sparkling Jewel. Though she would travel far from the Magic Sphere, the Sparkling Jewel would help Air keep her magical powers.

Air knew that her king would be proud of her accomplishments. She had met every challenge with bravery and strength. She had joined with her comrades, Earth and Water, in saving the Green Lord and his realm from death and destruction. She had helped to break the power of the Enchanter and to reveal his true form. And she had gained wisdom and understanding from the power of the Magic Sphere.